# A Stroke of Evil

# A Stroke of Evil

by

**Erica E. Remer, M.D.**

*Hope this is as close as you get to an emergency department!*

*Erica Remer*

Copyright © 2000 by Erica E. Remer

All rights reserved.
No part of this book may be reproduced, stored in a retrieval system, or transmitted by any means, electronic, mechanical, photocopying, recording, or otherwise, without written permission from the author.

**ISBN:** 1-58721-465-2

Image on cover from *Imaging of CNS Disease, second edition,* Douglas H. Yock, JR., Mosby Year Book, p. 333, 1991

1stBook – rev. 05/25/00

# ABOUT THE BOOK

"The radiographs were identical down to every curve and indentation of the brain matter. *That's impossible*, Elise thought, *that would be like two sets of identical fingerprints.*"

And thus, while preparing for a teaching conference, Dr. Elise Silver, chief emergency medicine resident, serendipitously discovers evidence of the unnatural death of Jefferey Weber, an elderly trustee of Chicago General Hospital. Her investigation to find the murderer brings her close to his handsome grandson, despite the fact that he is one of her prime suspects. Multiple medical vignettes reminiscent of the popular television show, *ER,* make this novel a quick paced and entertaining read. But will the lovely doctor meet her own untimely demise when she discovers the reason for Mr. Weber's stroke of evil?

# CHAPTER 1

"I think I have a case of child abuse in Room Six," Neil Anderson, M.D. whispered to his supervising resident.

"Hang on, just let me ask Jodi for the papers to enter Room Two in the niclodipine-stroke study," Elise replied as she approached the clerk's desk, her hand outstretched.

"Already stamped and ready, doc. Do you have your money for the pool?" the clerk asked.

"I think I'll pass this week. I figure the lottery won't be worth more than five million after that lucky son-of-a-gun cleaned up the thirty-eight million-dollar jackpot last weekend. Let me know when the jackpot goes over ten million, I'll go in again. Thanks for the papers."

Elise placed the papers on Room Two's clipboard and set it in the chart rack. She turned her attention to the intern to listen to his presentation.

Elise Silver, M.D. was a five foot two inch bundle of energy, which made her perfectly suited for her chosen profession. Her emerald green eyes were as observant as they were beautiful and she had high cheekbones and full lips. Short auburn hair which was naturally wavy and had a sprinkling of strands of gray was left untouched in the hopes that it would make her look older and more credible. Her powder blue lab coat could not hide the figure which belied her dedication to staying active despite the heavy demands of residency.

"Okay, what have you got?"

The lanky intern began his presentation, "This is a thirty-eight month old white male without past medical history whose father states he was playing with Lenny, flipping him over, and, all of a sudden, Lenny started crying inconsolably. Now he refuses to move that arm. Dad states he thinks he 'accidentally' broke his arm."

The emergency medicine residents had been given a lecture on child abuse in grand rounds three weeks previously. They were cautioned to be suspicious of stories that didn't jive, of delayed presentation to the emergency department, of certain patterns of injury like small circular burns or welts in the shape of a belt buckle. They were instructed that it was their moral and legal responsibility to report even suspected abuse, and let the authorities sort out the facts.

"I think we should get DCFS involved," he concluded.

Elise smiled knowingly after hearing Neil's textbook description of a common childhood problem. "Let's not call the police and department of children and family services in just yet."

The two training doctors entered Room Six. Lenny, a blond-haired, blue-eyed cherub, was perched on his father's lap. He burst into tears the moment he saw the ominous people dressed in lab coats with stethoscopes draped around their necks approach him. He clutched his father with his right arm, but his left arm lay limp at his side.

Elise began to talk to the boy in a high pitched, but soothing, voice. Neil thought to himself it was like watching a snake charmer weaving and bobbing in front of a king cobra's basket.

"Hey, peanut, what hurts? Boy, are you a big boy. And you have such beautiful eyes. Where'd you get those blond curls?" she chattered.

The experienced eyes of the third year resident quickly surveyed the child. He seemed to interact normally with his dad who, in turn, seemed duly concerned. His Osh Kosh B'Gosh navy shorts outfit and skin were soiled just as one would expect of an active child his age. There were several small bruises over his knees and shins consistent with being a toddler, but no lesions to suggest cigarette burns or whippings. She scrutinized his left arm; there was no area of swelling or deformity to hint at a broken bone. There was no reddening to suggest infection or an inflamed joint. In fact, as Elise had anticipated, there was no visible sign of any injury.

"Mister..." Elise glanced at the chart. "Stockton, could you please describe for us exactly what you two were doing when this happened?'

The frantic father demonstrated.

"I hold Lenny's hands and then he walks up my legs. When he gets to the top, he throws his legs back and does a flip. He usually laughs and asks for more. This time, he just started crying and wouldn't use his arm. I swear I didn't drop him, I don't know what happened!"

Neil was pretty pleased at his own vigilance. He regarded Mr. Stockton's protestations as evidence of his guilt. The intern found the area to order x-ray studies and marked off 'L elbow', writing, 'Rule out fracture' in the clinical information spot.

In the meantime, Elise palpated Lenny's left arm and confirmed her suspicion. She instructed the intern as she grasped Lenny's elbow with her left hand and his wrist and hand with her right hand.

"You want to stabilize the radial head with your thumb and then supinate and flex the arm until... voilá," she said as she performed the maneuver and felt the eminently satisfying click under her left thumb and Lenny began to wail.

"Mister Stockton, stop feeling guilty. Your son had a condition called 'nursemaid's elbow.' In fancy doctor terms, it is called *subluxation of the radial head*. It is very common in toddlers and it happens when there is a tug on the arm and one of the arm bones slips out from under its ligament. As we grow older, that bone flares out and it stays put." She explained as she drew a diagram on the bedsheet.

She turned her attention to the sniffling child, who was now eyeing her suspiciously, "Guess what, lamb chop, we don't even need x-rays!"

Neil shrugged and drew a single line through his order, writing next to it, 'Error' and his initials. He looked at his resident expectantly.

She turned back to Neil.

"In fact, if you had sent Lenny to radiology for a film, the x-ray tech would have had all the fun. By the time we saw him again, he'd have been acting like that and you would have been really perplexed!"

Neil looked back at the toddler. He had already forgotten his traumatic ordeal. He was now laughing and trying intently to climb up his father in order to reach behind him to grasp the black curly oto-ophthalmoscope cord. Neil marveled that he was using both his arms again.

"Sir, I would give Lenny a sling to buff my chart, but I think it would be a waste of Blue Cross' money. Just be careful when you are playing with him; children who have had this happen once are more likely to have it happen again. Please wait and the nurse will bring you in some instructions and sign you out. Do you have any questions?"

"Doctor, what if it does happen again?" Mr. Stockton answered.

"Try doing what I did," and she demonstrated on the doting dad's arm. "If all else fails, come on back. It's my favorite thing to do in the whole world, next to sleeping."

Elise rummaged through her pockets and selected a stegosaurus and a Pikachu Pokémon sticker and held them out to the towhead who accepted them eagerly. Elise had been instrumental in declaring Chicago General Hospital Emergency Department a Barney and Teletubbie-free zone, but other characters were fair game. One of Elise's crowning achievements of her medical student career was learning which Power Ranger was which. However, as soon as she had that down pat, they fell out of vogue and new characters replaced them in the hearts and minds of the American young. It was so hard keeping current on the important things.

"Thank you so much, doctor!" Mr. Stockton said, "Say goodbye, Lenny."

Elise laughed as she envisioned the little boy saying, "Good-bye, Lenny" in Gracie Allen's voice. They walked out as Lenny waved bye-bye.

Elise turned to Neil as they exited the exam room and reassured him, "Don't worry, it just takes time. You have to see lots of patients and you certainly will in this emergency department!

Nursemaid's elbow is a perfect example of why I picked emergency medicine. It gives you immediate satisfaction - a kid is in pain and you can actually fix him. I'll tell you, after twenty-five years of delayed gratification, it feels great."

Elise detoured past the clerk's desk and grabbed the chart for Room Two.

Jodi waved her down to attract her attention.

"Elise, Sid Shulman is in Room Two," she warned quietly.

*Doctor Shulman? Why would the president of the hospital be down here?* Elise wondered. She looked the chart over. There was a stamp up in the right hand corner which said, "V.I.P." That was usually reserved for trustees and big time supporters of the hospital as well as community bigwigs. The name, Jefferey Weber, didn't ring a bell with Elise, so he was probably one of the former.

"Isn't he going to speak in a hospital-wide forum on H.M.O.s in a couple of weeks? I think I remember getting a memo in the mail," Elise asked.

"Yeah. I'm sure it's bound to be bad news," Jodi responded.

"I heard C.G.H. is in trouble," Carol, one of the nurses loitering about the clerk's desk, added. "I hope that's just a rumor."

"Why don't you just ask Sid now and report back to us?" Jodi suggested jokingly.

"Not!" Elise said emphatically. She composed herself and walked to Room Two. The resident pulled back the vertically striped curtain and entered.

"Mister Weber, I'm Doctor Silver, the senior resident working with Doctor Anderson," she introduced herself.

She eyed the robust eighty-one year old man lying on the gurney. He was sitting straight upright in bed, feeling quite exposed and more than a bit foolish in the pale yellow hospital gown. His face was contorted with his mouth twisted, and his brown eyes were clouded and worried. He clutched the siderails of his gurney and his knuckles were white from the tension.

"Doctor Shulman," she nodded her head in greeting. "And who might this be?" she asked conversationally.

She motioned to the handsome, dark haired man seated beside Mr. Weber. He was wearing a pale tan shirt and an expensive looking silk tie.

*I love men wearing colored dress shirts*, Elise thought to herself. *And he reminds me a little of a young, thin Alec Baldwin with that thick dark hair and striking icy blue eyes. In fact, I've seen him before. Where?*

For a second, a distracted, faraway look came over her. Her near-photographic memory kicked in and she remembered the scene vividly.

It was several months previously. In Room Four, there was a demented old man who the paramedics had brought in off the streets. He had been found wandering near the sub shoppe where the medical boys in blue were grabbing lunch, and no family had been located as yet. He was unkempt and quite confused, but had no real complaints of pain. His physical examination showed some weakness of his left arm, which the gentleman stated was old.

Frustrated, Elise ordered everything imaginable on him, affectionately termed *the veterinary work-up*. The wisdom of this became apparent when Elise noticed that Mr. Krysewski said, "Yes" to *any* question asked of him.

Since it was still during bankers' hours, Elise walked over to Radiology to look over the C.T. scan of the brain with the neuroradiologist. Finally, Mr. Krysewski's behavior was understandable, as the female physician pointed out the area just next to the brain where there was a collection of old blood. It was a subtle finding, because the blood blended in with the brain tissue on the x-ray images.

"Will you be ready for lunch soon, Linda?" a deep voice called out from the threshold.

Elise and the neuroradiologist reflexively turned and saw him in the doorway.

"Thanks a lot!" Elise said as she collected the films off the illuminated reading screen to ultimately deliver to the neurosurgeon. "Have a good day."

"You, too. I'll be right there, Eric," Linda responded to her visitor.

It was only a momentary encounter, but he was attractive enough that it made an impression on the single resident. There was a faint hint of some unidentifiable, but luscious smelling, cologne as Elise passed him in the hallway.

Elise recalled a twinge of envy as she bemoaned the fact that she seemed unable to meet men like him. Fortunately, Mr. Krysewski fared better than her love life. When his niece came to the E.D., she explained that her uncle had deteriorated in the past three weeks, and, no, he had never had a stroke that they knew of. After the surgeons removed the blood from the surface of his brain, he returned back to his normal, non-confused, and perfectly symmetric, state.

Elise's attention returned to the present as Mr. Weber replied in a slurred voice, "This is my grandson, Eric."

He then looked her over and asked, "Are you married, young lady?"

Elise playfully rolled her eyes. "Your chart must be mistaken. It says 'retired' under the entry for occupation. Should it read '*yenta*'?"

Mr. Weber laughed heartily and Elise sensed she had established rapport as his body language heralded relaxation. She noted out of the corner of her eye that the handsome grandson was actually blushing.

The president of the hospital reached over the siderail and took Mr. Weber's hand. He gave it a reassuring squeeze.

"Jeff, I'm going to leave you in this capable young doctor's hands. I'll plan on seeing you at the club next week. Let's do dinner," Mr. Shulman said.

"Okay, Sid. Thanks for stopping down to see me," Mr. Weber said slowly.

After Dr. Shulman had left, Elise began verifying information, "Now then, I understand before today your only medical problems were a heart valve replacement, high blood pressure, and prostate trouble."

"My eyes ain't too good and I hear better out of my right ear, but I'm not bad for a guy my age," Mr. Weber quipped.

"The nurse documented that you take Vasotec, Coumadin, and Dyazide and you have no allergies."

"PopPop, you're allergic to ragweed," Eric interjected.

"Shah, she means to drugs," his grandfather corrected him.

Elise smiled. It was nice to see such attentiveness.

"My intern has told me a bit about you but let me just go over it with you. When did you get sick?"

Elise had to strain to decipher Mr. Weber's response because his speech was difficult to understand at times. His accent was reminiscent of her grandmother's; he probably hailed from Germany or Austria. She guessed he had either survived, or narrowly escaped being interred in, a concentration camp. His speech difficulty wasn't easy to identify either. It wasn't exactly dysarthria, a slurring of speech seen with certain types of strokes, but it also didn't seem to be the other common speech problem, dysphasia. Mr. Weber just seemed to be having trouble articulating his words at a normal pace.

"I took my medicine this morning when I got up. We ate breakfast, a little cereal, some fruit, coffee," *Why do old people always insist on sharing their menus with me?* Elise pondered, as she squelched a yawn born of sleep deprivation.

"and toast with just a touch of butter to it. I know I should avoid cholesterol, but you can't live forever. Around ten-thirty my face got twisted like this. I called Doc Tony at the office and he called the ambulance for me. I left Eric a note to meet me here."

Elise found the entry under 'attending physician'. Anthony Romano, M.D. was a well respected family practitioner who had grown up in the community and was a very active physician in the hospital as well as being on the board of trustees.

"I was in South Carolina on business and I just flew back in this morning," Mr. Weber's grandson offered in explanation.

"Doctor Silver, the orientee is here," a nurse interrupted by calling into the room.

"Okay, I'll be right out," Elise acknowledged.

She hurriedly performed a cursory physical examination and then said, "Mister Weber, Doctor Anderson and I have extensively discussed your case. We are concerned you may have had a stroke. We are going to need to do some tests, including a brain scan. I'd also like to leave you some material to read and I'll return to go over it with you. Here at Chicago General we often are involved in research that we believe may help present or future patients. Our department is currently involved in a study on a new medication called niclodipine. Its purpose is to try to minimize effects from a stroke. You may be a good candidate and we'd like you to consider participating. The paperwork will explain the risks and benefits thoroughly to you. I will be happy to answer any questions you have after you have read through it."

"That's one of the new calcium channel blockers, isn't it?" Eric asked.

Surprised, Elise answered, "Yes, it is. Are you in the medical profession?"

"I'm a chemist. I work for Clark-Davies. I try to keep up on new drugs, even if they aren't our products. You have to keep track of the competition, " he explained.

She handed the information packet and consent form to Mr. Weber and Eric stood to accept them.

"I'll read them to PopPop for you, doctor."

"Thanks, " she said as she thought a distinctly unprofessional thought about his light blue eyes and noticed the absence of a ring or a tan line on his left fourth finger. "I'll be back soon."


Richard Brewer was waiting patiently by the counter where the nurse had parked him. His dark brown eyes were bright and his mocha brown skin was unblemished and clean-shaven. Elise loved the sound of his deep voice as he introduced himself.

"Rich Brewer. I'm a fourth year medical student at Northwestern and I'm very interested in pursuing a career in emergency medicine," he said eagerly and extended his right hand to assertively shake Elise's.

"Elise Silver, I'm one of the senior residents this month and the chief asked me to orient you. Let me give you a quick tour of the department. We'll start in the lounge so I can grab my next cup of coffee."

She led him to the lounge and showed him the important features - the unisex bathroom, the fridge where scary, smelly green things grew and all food was fair game unless you clearly labeled your bag or container with your name and the date. He was shown the coffee can for contributions next to the coffee machine, the microwave (primarily for popcorn at three a.m.), and the bulletin board liberally scattered with the staff's babies' pictures and brochures on conferences.

"Your mailbox is over here and articles for journal club should be in there by Monday afternoon. Also if there are any operational memos or residency information, that is where they would be. If you find you need to rearrange your schedule, mark the changes on the master. Be sure to run any switches past the chief resident first, though. You will find the medical students' shifts are listed on the residents' schedule. Both the residents' and attendings' schedules are over here on the wall."

As they walked out into the department, coffee cups full, Elise prefaced her tour.

"Chicago General is a five hundred bed, not-for-profit hospital run by the Sacred Sisters of Charity located in the heart of metropolitan Chicago. The surrounding area has changed in recent years and you don't go near the windows from eleven-thirty p.m. to one a.m. on New Year's Eve or you might get shot at from the projects across the street. Nevertheless, there are excellent doctors and state-of-the-art medical programs. A large cross section of the Chicago population still utilizes our services. That's why it is perfectly suited to have an emergency medicine residency. Unlike the East Coast, where there are turf wars between surgery and medicine as to who should control the E.D., we are our own department here.

"We see about thirty-eight thousand patients per year and the less sick ones are siphoned off to the minor emergency area during day hours. Our patient population is approximately thirty percent pediatrics and the pathology is widely varied. We don't have a peds ICU so we transfer those patients to Wyler's or Children's. We also transfer burn patients. Other than that, we keep just about everyone. We are a designated trauma center, one of only six in the metropolitan Chicago area. Are you familiar with the concept of trauma centers?"

The medical student hesitantly shook his head in the negative.

"Studies have shown that places that see a lot of trauma, become more proficient at handling trauma. The EMS system is attuned to this. When they pick up a patient who has been involved in a car accident or has been shot, they run through criteria to determine whether the patient warrants a specialized trauma facility, or if they can be managed in any old hospital. If they should mistriage a patient, the receiving hospital will stabilize the patient as best they can, and then transfer the patient to an accepting trauma center."

The couple strode through the double doors to arrive in the waiting room area and Elise pointed, "Walk-in patients enter through there and present to the triage nurse here."

A cramped cubicle where a nurse was inflating a blood pressure cuff on an elderly patient was the first stop. She stopped for a moment and acknowledged the emergency medicine resident.

"Hi, Didi, don't mind us. This is Rich Brewer, a fourth year student from Northwestern."

Didi smiled warmly, "Welcome, Rich. My advice to you is, 'Chux are our friends.'" The triage nurse returned her attention to her patient, and Elise explained her words of wisdom.

"You'll find that here, as in many areas of the hospital, the nurses really run the show. If you get on their good side, they can be very helpful. If you piss the wrong one off, heaven help you! So, Didi was telling you to use those disposable liners, Chux, whenever you are likely to make a mess, and you will make friends with the nursing staff. I, personally, go a step further and bring in food. I call it *Purina nurse chow.*"

Rich laughed a deep throaty laugh.

"So the triage nurse determines the patient's chief complaint and takes vital signs and does a quick screening exam. The patient then either goes to registration first, over there, or he is expedited right back into the department if he has a potentially serious problem. The charts are then placed..."

Elise punched a metal plate on the wall and the double doors swung open into the bustling E.D. They walked through and Elise pointed at the chart rack.

"...here in order of severity of illness, not necessarily in order of arrival. That is one of the hardest things to explain to the irate masses outside, that the sickest are cared for first.

"The charge nurse will select a chart when a room is available and brings the patient back. The chart is then placed in that rack and flagged for the physician's attention. The charge nurse writes the patient's name and other data on the patient flow board on the wall over there. When you pick up a patient, sign your initials in the upper right hand corner and take the chart out of the box."

Elise showed the medical student the general layout of the main emergency department, with twelve examining rooms and four holding rooms arranged in a horseshoe shape surrounding the centralized nursing/charting station.

There was a single Trauma room and three additional rooms, Two through Four, which would house the most critically ill patients. Rooms Five through Eight were for intermediate acuity patients. Nine and Ten were the only rooms with actual doors, and this served to give the obstetrics/gynecology patients some privacy and to give the rest of the patients some peace and quiet when small, screaming children populated them. Room Eleven was the ear, nose and throat (ENT) room and contained specialized equipment to examine and treat those areas. Room Twelve, the Cast Room, was equipped for caring for fractures. The holding rooms were intended to hold patients as they awaited lab results or if they required re-examination before decisions were made.

The walls of the department were a pale rose color and the curtains were multi-colored in an attempt to camouflage any unsolicited body fluids that might splash on them. That distinctly antiseptic hospital smell abounded. Elise brought Rich into one of the few unoccupied cubicles and opened drawers and cabinets to expose the uniformly stocked supplies.

"Tongue depressors, Q-tips, stuff for rectals in this drawer. Respiratory supplies are here by the oxygen source. Linens are underneath, along with emesis basins, urinals, and bedpans," she said as she demonstrated their locations.

"Doctor Silver, there's a *Code R* in Room Ten, " Elise was informed by Janet through the curtain.

"I'll be right there, thanks, " Elise replied.

She turned to Rich, who looked just a tad overwhelmed. "We'll go over the discharge and admitting procedures as we need to dispose of patients. Any other questions?"

"No," he answered hesitantly. He had so many questions he didn't know where to begin!

She smiled reassuringly. "You'll be fine. Go, enjoy your day off. We'll see you tomorrow at one p.m."

He thanked the busy resident, collected his belongings and left to run errands. Elise took a deep cleansing breath in order to focus on her next task.

# CHAPTER 2

As she prepared to enter Room Ten, Elise shuddered. Like everyone else, she hated dealing with sexual assault victims, the politically correct term for *rape*. However, everyone assumed *Code R* victims preferred seeing a female physician, so Elise would probably see them all on the days when she was the only woman physician on duty. As sympathetic as she felt toward the patient, it was often difficult to contain her anger against such wanton violence.

Elise was glad to see Kathy, her favorite nurse, in the room. Kathy was taking information and trying to explain to the patient the procedures which would follow. She was a petite brunette with hazel eyes and a soft, soothing voice and manner. Elise was friends with Kathy and her husband, and Anna, Kathy's daughter, loved seeing Dr. Elise when she came to visit the E.D.

Kathy, on the other hand, was even happier to see Elise enter the room because Mrs. Garcia's English was only fair, at best. Elise's Spanish was at least adequate and she, therefore, was also dealt more than her fair share of Hispanic patients in the average day.

Elise took the chart and glanced at the triage note. It said: *Code R*. For the sake of confidentiality and privacy, it was not helpful.

She identified herself, "*Señora, soy la doctora* Silver. *¿Qué fue?*"

In a soft, tearful voice, the forty-one year old heavyset Mexican woman detailed the story of how, after her husband and three other children had left for work and school respectively, a tall, strong black man had jimmied open her apartment window and forced himself on her. She showed the marks on her face from where he slapped her when she screamed. He had brandished a pistol and threatened to kill her and her three-year-old daughter if she resisted any further.

Elise murmured reassurances she had done just the right thing and that everything was going to be okay. But she knew that it would be a very long time before mentally and emotionally Mrs. Garcia would be okay again. Elise ascertained that her child had been unharmed and was being watched by a neighborhood friend. She asked about condom use and whether there was any oral or anal penetration. She inquired about ejaculation and asked when Mrs. Garcia's last consensual intercourse was.

The resident then began her physical examination. She explained how she would first examine the entire body and then focus on her female parts. At that point, Elise noted several abraded and tender areas in the vagina consistent with unlubricated entry.

*Good, at least I'll have some ammunition in court*, she thought.

There was semen in the vagina and Elise took specimens which she would quickly examine to see if she found sperm, especially moving ones. Elise noted the cervix looked bluish and bled easily when samples were taken to check for venereal disease.

"*Señora, ¿quantas veces estaba embarazada?*"

Mrs. Garcia replied she had been pregnant four times.

Elise did her bimanual examination, which supported her suspicion. Mrs. Garcia answered her next question that she hadn't had a period in three months. Mrs. Garcia assumed she was beginning the change of life.

Elise stripped her gloves off and washed the talc off her hands. She carefully handed the specimens she had collected to Kathy who labeled and processed each one.

"Kathy, please get the usuals and have the evidence tech take pictures. Let me know when you're done with the pregnancy test."

The female police officer asked if she could enter as Elise exited. Elise inquired if they had caught the slime mold who had done it. She was told they did have some leads and they actually did expect to catch the perpetrator.

In terms of justice, Elise was thrilled. However, the implication for her was that she would receive a summons expecting her to drop everything, including shift responsibilities, to appear in court to testify. There were frequently postponements at the last minute. It was always very aggravating, especially since she had such a legible handwriting and her dictations were so thorough that her charts should have been able to stand on their own. *Oh well*, at least maybe she could help prevent a repeat assault.

A detour to the dirty utility room, which also housed the microscope, revealed motile sperm. Pleased with herself, Elise went into the lounge to grab another cup of coffee.

Chicago General's emergency department was known to have the best java around and that was one of the main reasons it was constantly inundated with ambulances. The paramedics appreciated quality. However, they appreciated quantity more, and there were always doughnut holes, pretzels, candy, or other assorted junk foods around.

Her caffeine craving satiated, Elise walked back to Room Two to finish her exam and explain the research project more thoroughly. She was a bit startled to see the gurney missing. Neil informed her that he had discussed the study with Mr. Weber and his grandson and he was willing to be included.

"I believe his exact words were, 'Doctor, I am your obedient guinea pig.'"

He further reported that the necessary blood specimens had been drawn and Mr. Weber had been wheeled to the C.T. scan room in the department of Radiology.

"I even contacted Doctor Romano to notify him that his patient was in the E.D."

"Good job," praised his senior resident. "It's past one-thirty. Have you eaten yet?"

"Yeah, I brought a sandwich. I'm not sure what it was because I gobbled it down so fast, but I'm sure it was good for me. My wife packs my lunches," Neil admitted sheepishly.

"I wish I had a wife," Elise said wistfully.

There was always a low grade hum of voices in the E.D. (the term, 'emergency room' or 'E.R.' was shunned by the specialists of emergency medicine as a throwback to the days when just anyone with a medical degree staffed the area) which often swelled to a roar, punctuated frequently by the overhead hospital-wide intercom system. An attending physician was present twenty-four hours a day and would be board certified in emergency medicine because C.G.H. was home to the three year emergency medicine residency. Except for the hours of five a.m. to seven a.m., there was at least one resident seeing patients as well. Medical students from schools in the Chicagoland area rotated at four to six week intervals as well. Four to six emergency nurses, a patient care technician, one to two registration clerks, an orders' clerk, and a billing person rounded off the personnel list. At any given time, representatives from lab, x-ray, housekeeping, and the respiratory department might also be found milling about. Consultants from other specialties, like surgery or pediatrics, were also available if their services were required in the care of a patient. The final contributors to the tumult were the patients themselves and their friends or family members.

Kathy signaled to Elise to attract her attention without having to add to the din and Elise walked over to join her at the nurses' station. The pretty nurse handed her Mrs. Garcia's chart with the lab results attached.

Elise looked them over and said, "I figured as much. Well, at least I don't have to go through the old Ovral speech."

Mrs. Garcia looked much older than her forty-one years, Elise observed as she reentered Room Ten.

"*Señora, no ha tenido su menstruación porque ya está embarazada.*" Elise continued to tell her she would take medicine to prevent infection, but since Mrs. Garcia was already pregnant, medication need not be dispensed to prevent conception. Counseling about H.I.V. testing was done and the patient opted to get checked. The sexual assault crisis worker would give Mrs. Garcia emotional support and referral literature in Spanish to meet her future needs.

The next patient was a twenty-two year old man accompanied by his girlfriend.

"Doctor, Seth is not a complainer. The only other time he was in the emergency room was for a broken ankle that needed surgery and it took him thirty-six hours to be convinced to get it checked out! He has been feeling awful since last night around dinnertime, and I didn't even have to plead with him to see a doctor. He asked me to take him here," the girlfriend explained.

"Mister Marcus, what exactly made you ask to come in?" Elise explored.

"I started having a stomachache after dinner. I guess the leftover chicken was no good," he said, giving his friend a dirty look.

"Why are you looking at me?! I ate it too and I'm fine, " the woman protested. She turned to Elise and added, "He's such a brat. If the expiration date on the milk is two days away, he doesn't want to drink it. He hates eating leftovers, but I didn't feel like cooking. So sue me!"

"Anyway, around two a.m., I woke up vomiting. The pain has become pretty severe. The ride over pretty much sucked," he admitted.

"Why?" Elise asked even though she suspected she knew what his response would be.

"Every bump in the road gave me sharp pains."

"Yeah, if he wasn't so sick, I'd be pissed. He kept accusing me of being a lousy female driver!" his girlfriend said with a tender smile.

Elise scanned the chart for the triage nurse's recording of his vital signs. "When did you start running a fever?" she asked when she noted a temperature of 38.7 ° C. Elise had not grown up with the metric system so she still had a tendency to perform the calculations necessary to convert temperature into something she could relate to. Mr. Marcus had a fever of 101.7 ° F.

"I didn't know I had a fever," he answered.

"I told you you were sick!" his girlfriend interjected.

"Tell me this, what is your favorite food in the whole world?" Elise asked the pale patient.

"Doc, right now you couldn't force me to eat if you threatened my life. I would puke right on you," he said as he winced from a wave of pain.

Elise set her chart down on the counter and approached Mr. Marcus, rubbing her hands together to try to warm them up before she touched his abdomen.

"I'm going to examine you now. Then we will get some tests and try to figure out what is wrong with you."

Mr. Marcus' physical examination was only interesting for one finding. He was exquisitely tender in the right part of his lower abdomen. When Elise pressed in and then released, Seth yelped.

"Mister Marcus, I am very concerned that you have an inflamed appendix. I would like to draw some labs on you and we will start an I.V. at the same time. When was the last time you ate or drank anything?"

"Ugh, you're talking about food again," he responded.

"Honey, you tried drinking some juice at around eight o'clock, but it came back up," Seth's companion pointed out.

"Alright, well, don't eat or drink anything from here on out until I tell you it's okay," Elise cautioned him. "You very well may need surgery and it's been about eight hours since you last had something by mouth. You should have an empty stomach if you have to go to the O.R. The surgeons will be by to evaluate you shortly."

As she left the room, Elise jotted down her orders on the chart to give to the clerk. When Jodi paged her overhead, Elise told Mr. Marcus' story to the general surgery resident who promised to be down to evaluate him shortly.

"Hey, Neil, go talk to the people in Room Seven and tell me what you think," Elise suggested.

Fifteen minutes later, Neil caught up with Elise and gave her his opinion, "Man, he couldn't have a more classic presentation of appendicitis! It's like he read the textbook."

"Good job," Elise praised him. "Let's see what the surgeons think. Sometimes I think they disagree with me just to be contrary."

Elise was duly impressed with Neil's knowledge base and ability to synthesize, especially considering it was only the middle of August. She warned her loved ones to avoid being hospitalized in July since all the doctors are brand spanking new at their respective jobs. Fortunately, since the field of emergency medicine was so competitive, the selected interns were usually the cream of the crop and very attuned to the way emergency medicine people think.

"I need a doctor in Room Two, *STAT!*" bellowed a nurse.

Elise's heart pounded. In this department, the nurses were extremely independent and competent. If they needed someone *STAT*, they meant *right now*!

She burst into Room Two to find Mr. Weber in complete cardiac arrest. The room was instantly filled with personnel, each of whom knew his or her job and performed it without hesitation.

Jackie pulled Mr. Weber's gown up and reconnected the monitor leads to the electrodes on his chest to check his heart rhythm. Alyssa, the respiratory therapist who just happened to be administering a breathing treatment to a little girl in Room Eight, assumed a position at the head of the bed and began bagging Mr. Weber, pumping oxygen into his lungs.

"While we are getting him hooked up, could someone please begin C.P.R.?" Elise requested in a carefully controlled voice.

Steven Joynt, an orderly who was in the process of completing his premedical requirements, began chest compressions at Elise's solicitation. He found the bottom of the breastbone and positioned his hands appropriately. He began rhythmically pushing the chest in and releasing. Alyssa got into his rhythm and inserted breaths every fifth compression.

Neil was assisting Elise prepare for intubation. Mr. Weber was not breathing on his own so he needed a tube down his windpipe to provide a direct passage to his lungs. As Elise checked the balloon and inserted the guide wire into the tube, she asked in a decisive voice, "Do we have anything on the monitor?"

It was flat line - no electrical activity. Elise ordered epinephrine and atropine intravenously and proceeded to remove Mr. Weber's dentures. She told Steve to resume C.P.R.

"Neil, what are possible causes of asystole?" Elise asked didactically.

"Hypoxia, hyperkalemia, acidosis, um, hypothermia," his voice trailed off as he tried to recall the other reasons for the heart to stop beating.

Steve offered, "Certain kinds of drug overdoses."

"Good, Steve. Neil, you mentioned too much potassium. Hypokalemia can also cause asystole," the senior resident completed the list.

Elise inserted the laryngoscope into Mr. Weber's mouth and lifted up his tongue and lower jaw. She then expertly inserted the endotracheal tube between the vocal cords and held the tube tightly in place. Neil confirmed the placement in the right spot by listening over the lungs and abdomen as Jackie squeezed oxygen in and they checked the end-tidal $CO_2$ monitor. He reported that it seemed like it was in good position.

"Do we have anything yet?" Elise asked authoritatively.

Alyssa secured the endotracheal tube with special tape around Mr. Weber's lips. The respiratory therapist then took over the job of bagging again and began to hyperventilate. Elise called out to Jodi to order a portable chest x-ray to double-check the tube placement.

The monitor hadn't changed. Kathy, who was recording all the events, reported it had been three minutes since the first round of meds. Elise ordered an escalated dose of epinephrine and another ampule of atropine. She checked Mr. Weber's pupils. He had dense cataracts bilaterally, but the pupils were dilated and did not react to light.

"Neil, what do you make of his pupils?"

He inspected the eyes and concluded, "I don't think he's going to make it."

"Unfortunately, I agree," Elise replied, "but you can't make anything of pupillary response, or lack thereof, after two milligrams of atropine. The drug itself will dilate the pupils and can be misleading."

Dr. Weinfeld, the attending, entered the room holding a set of C.T. films. He flipped on the viewbox lights and positioned the x-rays. From across the room, Elise could see their attempts were destined to be futile. Mr. Weber had sustained a huge intracranial hemorrhage which was just not compatible with life.

"Steve, hold C.P.R.," Elise instructed the sweating patient care technician. "We left out death on our list. Death causes asystole, too."

As expected, there was still nothing on the monitor. The senior resident quickly ran through the formal process of pronouncing a patient deceased. Elise looked at the clock and announced, "We're calling it at four twenty-seven p.m. Thank you everyone for all your help."

Elise looked at Neil and told him in a quiet voice that he should practice intubation. Getting experience when speed was not crucial meant being able to perform the life-saving procedure when it really could make a difference. She watched his first attempt with approval and then left the room to find Eric Weber. Although she deplored the circumstances, she had to admit she didn't dread the prospect of seeing him again.

"Jodi, can you get Doctor Romano on the line for me? He probably will sign the death certificate," Elise said.

"It may be a little while. He was here in the department just a little bit ago. On his way out, he told me he was leaving the hospital. I can usually reach him on his cellular phone, though. If not, I'll page him," the clerk responded.

She was surprised to find Mr. Weber's grandson was neither in the quiet room nor the waiting room. She took a deep breath and hoped she wouldn't find him amidst the tobacco- addicted people congregating outside the E.D. doors.

When she remarked on her inability to locate him, Jackie stated that the grandson had told her he needed to go into his laboratory for a short while, but that he said he'd be back soon.

Dr. Romano answered his page promptly and Elise took the call. He told her he would sign the death certificate.

"Mister Weber has been a friend and a patient of mine for many years. I can't believe he's gone." Elise was touched by the way his voice cracked and she could feel tears welling up in her own eyes.

She made a mental note to call her grandmother as soon as she got home.


At five-fifteen p.m., Kathy pulled Elise out of a room to tell her Eric had returned and was in the quiet room. Pastoral care had been summoned and would arrive shortly.

Elise knocked and entered. Eric was sitting on the sofa and when he saw the solemn look on her face, he intuited, "You have bad news."

Elise sat next to him and explained the unexpected course of events. She assured him that his grandfather had not suffered and that everything had been done to try to save him.

"I just can't believe he's gone. He seemed fine when I left him on his way to C.T. He told me to bring him some halvah tonight when I came to visit." Eric absently motioned to a small white bag from a well-known local delicatessen.

The hospital chaplain entered and sat on the other side of Eric. He comforted him and when Elise excused herself, he was explaining the procedure which would follow. Since the cause of death was clear, and Dr. Romano was willing to sign the death certificate, Elise was sure the coroner would release the body without an autopsy. She assured the grandson that Mr. Weber would be able to be buried within twenty-four hours in accordance with Jewish law.

Elise's shift ended at seven p.m. and she was pensive on her ride home. She hated losing patients and would often repeatedly mentally review unsuccessful codes to see if anything should have been done differently. She finally conceded that sometimes, no matter what you do, you can't change the outcome. *Mr. Weber had a fatal bleed. That's why they call hypertension the silent killer,* she thought, *and being on a blood thinner sealed his fate.*


At home, Elise kicked her shoes off and curled up on the couch in her cozy one bedroom apartment. She scratched her black cat, Fluffers, behind his ears as she opened her mail. She picked out a pink envelope which looked personal, as opposed to all the junk mail stamped "personal and confidential" which was neither.

"You are cordially invited to a baby shower for Ronna Peebles," Elise read on an invitation sprinkled with festive farm animals. Laura Peebles was a recent graduate from Elise's residency program and had stayed on as an attending. Elise was friendly with her as well as her husband, Carl. They had been having infertility grief and had recently purchased an eight-week-old puppy of husky and Dalmatian mix to fill that void. Elise shrugged and, although she thought it odd to have a shower for a dog, she realized emergency health care workers would make any excuse for a party.

After she had paid and filed the bills and disposed of the trash, she sat back down on the couch and dialed the long distance number. The phone rang four or five times. Finally the familiar voice answered.

"Hello?"

"Hey, Grandma, how are you doing?"

"*Schlepping* along. How are you? Have you found a husband yet?"

*Husband, I haven't even had a decent date in months*, Elise thought disgustedly. Men tended to find female physicians intimidating, and Elise could put off the best of them. She was very strong-willed, although she was genuinely receptive to others' ideas and opinions. She spoke her mind and strongly admired honesty in her partner. Her major problem in developing relationships was also her strong point - she did everything with such intensity that it could be terrifying to a man who was anything short of totally secure with himself.

"No, Grandma. You're going to have to stick around a while longer to walk down the aisle at my wedding. How's the rheumatism?"

"You tell me, you're the doctor. *Nu*, you are still in the emergency room?"

Elise had given up trying to explain this to her grandmother. She just couldn't understand the concept of a doctor not having a practice and private patients. But where else would you want someone who was specially trained more than in the emergency department where quick decisions were necessary all the time?

"Yes, Grandma. How's the weather there?"

They chatted for a few more minutes and then ended their call.

"This is costing you a bundle of money."

"I love you, Grandma."

"I love you, *mamaleh*. More than you'll ever know."

Elise picked the remote control up off the coffee table. Clicking past any program with a medical theme, she finally settled on a good science fiction flick on Showtime. She popped a Healthy Dinner in the microwave and ate it mindlessly in front of the television set. This was one consolation for being romantically unattached. No need to spend lots of time cooking a gourmet meal. Able to eat in front of the boob tube without having to make conversation. Able to relax and unwind her own way.

Two and a half hours later, the heroine had saved the world from the aliens yet again. Elise dragged her weary body and mind into her bedroom, and prepared for bed. Fluffers cuddled up beside her and Elise hoped for pleasant dreams. If she couldn't have that, she hoped for no dreams at all.

# CHAPTER 3

"Missus Connolly is back from x-ray and she's still having severe pain," Nancy, a tall, blonde nurse who had recently transferred down from the oncology floor, informed Elise.

Elise reviewed the intravenous pyelogram with the medical student, Richard Brewer. She furrowed her brow.

"The I.V.P. doesn't show kidney stones. The scout film they took before they injected the dye didn't show gallstones and there was no free air to indicate a perforated ulcer. But she is really having severe pain. If she were older, I'd be thinking about a *AAA*. I wish our radiology department routinely did spiral C.T. for stones. Cheap nuns. But I'm really at a loss."

Rich looked at her quizzically, "What's a *triple-A*?"

"An abdominal aortic aneurysm. As people get older, especially if they have atherosclerosis, there can be a weakening of the wall of the aorta, the biggest blood vessel in the body. It can balloon out and even burst. If it does that, it can be catastrophic. You'd like to catch it before then, even before it is just leaking," she explained. "Maybe I'll have surgery evaluate her."

She turned to the desk and asked the orders' clerk, Michelle, to get the surgical resident on the phone.

"I'll be in Room Nine."

Michelle liked working with Elise. The resident always kept her informed and was clear about her orders. She could even forgive the fact that Elise had a tendency to add tests after Michelle had already cleared the patient's order input screen. Elise could get crabby if the department got out of control, but she respected the nurses' opinions, was very thorough, and really cared about the patients. Everyone felt the same way about her - she could be a royal pain to work with sometimes, but if one of their family members was ill, she was the one they wanted handling the case.

Elise read the triage note as she knocked on the door, *'Seventeen year old complaining of multiple symptoms.'* The pregnancy test and urinalysis results were already clipped on the chart. At Chicago General, if you were female, of menstruating age, and you still owned a uterus, you had a pregnancy test performed, usually before you ever made it into an examining room.

"Tawanna, I'm Doctor Silver. What seems to be the problem today?"

The young woman looked at Elise with big brown eyes. "I been using it a lot."

"Does it burn when you pee?"

Elise expected the negative reply.

"Does your stomach hurt?"

"No."

"Have you been throwing up?"

"Yeah, I vomicks all the time."

"Well, Tawanna, your pregnancy test is positive. Have you been using any birth control?"

"No."

As she examined the child-like patient, Elise subjected Tawanna to her standard safe sex speech. In this day and age, unprotected sex not only resulted in pregnancy, but in sexually transmitted diseases, including AIDS. It was ironic; in the old days, you would implore patients to give up cigarettes and booze and take up sex. But nothing was safe anymore!

Tawanna had a few questions, "But I'm tired all the time."

"Yes, you're pregnant."

"And how come my boobs be so sore?"

"You're *pregnant*!" Elise said exasperatedly.

Elise wrote a prescription for prenatal vitamins and recommended prompt follow-up with the obstetrics clinic for prenatal care. She shook her head as she walked out. Actually, many of her first time mothers-to-be were much younger than Tawanna. *Babies having babies*, she thought.

The twenty-nine year old resident wanted a family someday but her parents were old fashioned - they expected her to get married first.

She walked back into Room Six to reevaluate Mrs. Connolly. The surgical resident was in there and had just begun his evaluation. As he pulled up the patient's robe to inspect her abdomen, the physicians could see five small blisters in a row overlying her right flank where her pain was.

"I can't believe it!" Elise exclaimed. "I swear those weren't there three hours ago when I first saw her."

The surgical resident gave her a devilish look and replied dubiously, "Yeah, sure. Can I go now or do you still want a surgical consult?"

Elise sheepishly dismissed him and called Rich in.

"What is your assessment?"

Rich looked questioningly at her and offered, "Herpes?"

In explanation, Elise said, "Missus Connolly, I am relieved that we now know what is causing your pain. You have shingles; the fancy medical name for it is *Herpes zoster.* It is caused by the exact same virus which gives kids the chicken pox. The virus hides in the nerve root and comes out along its path, often at a time of stress. It's not dangerous, but it certainly can be painful. We will prescribe some medication for you and you should follow-up with your doctor. Return if you see signs of infection. Also, be careful not to be around people who haven't had the chicken pox before. They could get it from you in this condition."

"How long am I contagious for? I'm a nursery school teacher," Mrs. Connolly said.

"Not for the next few weeks, you aren't. You're contagious until all of the blisters are scabbed over," Elise answered. "I hope you have some sick days coming."


As she dictated the case and wrote up discharge papers, the telemetry alarm sounded. One of the most frustrating things about emergency medicine was it was very difficult to complete any task without interruption. It is one of the few fields in medicine where multiple patients are evaluated simultaneously instead of consecutively.

She overheard the nurse repeating the report, "...term delivery. *ETA* two minutes."

She instructed Michelle to page the OB-Gyne and Pediatrics residents and invite them down to join the fun. Monica Sheehan, R.N. adjusted the incubator and took out an emergency delivery kit. She put on a pair of sterile gloves and began laying out the instruments.

True to their word, two minutes later the paramedics burst through the glass doors with a hugely obese woman holding a glistening newborn on her chest swaddled in a silver foil blanket to keep in the warmth.

Mike guided the head of the gurney in the OB room and began telling Elise the information, "This is Stella Grayson. She is thirty-six years old and gravida five, para five, at least she is now. She has been having irregular bleeding on and off throughout this entire pregnancy."

"Doc, I didn't even know I was pregnant!" Mrs. Grayson wailed.

*And I can't figure out HOW you got pregnant, you are so humongous*, Elise thought to herself rudely.

The resident had heard many stories of nebulous doctors at some other institution who had delivered full term babies from women who were unaware they were pregnant. She always had found it hard to believe. *Just when you thought you had seen it all...*

"I've always been fat. I just thought I was shrinking my pants in the wash. You would think after four pregnancies, I would feel pregnant. I just felt tired," she said. "He's pretty cute, isn't he? But where the hell did he get that red hair from? Boy, is my husband going to get the surprise of his life when he finds out about this!"

The paramedics informed Elise that the patient had been sitting out on the porch after calling 911 for abdominal pain.

"It felt like such bad cramps," Mrs. Grayson clarified.

Elise muttered sarcastically under her breath, "You mean like labor pains?"

Mike took Elise aside after the entire medical personnel moved the huge woman onto the gyne cart. He finished telling her the story privately.

"She started screaming, 'I have to take a shit! I have to take a shit!' and then her face scrunched up and got red. Then she started yelling, 'Something's coming out!' So I pulled off her filthy, bloody underwear and looked. Hair! Red freakin' hair! I yelled up front, 'She's having a baby!' and delivered him. His Apgars were eight and nine. How much you think he weighs?"

Elise unwrapped the infant while Michael told her the story. She dried the wriggling neonate off with warm towels and examined him under the incubator warming lights. He seemed full term to her. Furthermore, he seemed to be squirming with a purpose.

"Ha, you can't get me!" she declared triumphantly as she deftly intercepted his first stream of urine with a towel. It was a personal goal of hers never to be sprayed again. She answered Michael, "He looks at least eight pounds to me. The L&D nurses will weigh him officially."

"Well, what's his name going to be?" Monica queried as she filled out the hospital birth certificate and namebands. It offended her sensibilities to write 'Baby Boy Grayson.'

Mrs. Grayson's right arm shot out suddenly and grabbed the paramedic who had been driving, by the shirt, startling him. She inspected his nametag, and then replied, "Michael Luis Grayson."

Everyone laughed, especially Mike and Luis. They handed Monica their ambulance run sheet and stepped out to grab a cup of fine C.G.H. coffee before they had to hit the streets again. Elise overheard Luis griping about always having to take second billing as they exited the room.

"Boy, that kid should be glad Mad Dog Sullivan wasn't working that rig today!" Monica quipped.

As the consulting residents arrived, Elise relinquished both patients to their respective caregivers and completed the paperwork for admission. Although deliveries were messy and could be disruptive to the department, they were usually fun (more fun if you actually got to *do* the delivering) and rewarding. It was so exciting to bring a new baby into the world.

There were a bunch of loose ends to tie up before the end of her shift. Elise checked Mr. Killiam's ankle films. She walked back into Room Six to share the good news that it was just a minor sprain. Pam was applying a bandage to his right shoulder where he had sustained an abrasion when his bicycle wiped out on the road.

"Hey, doc, could you write me a prescription for those nicotine patches? They've worked miracles for me," Mr. Killiam implored.

Elise wrinkled her forehead, and her eyes quickly resurveyed Mr. Killiam's torso. She couldn't see patch anywhere on his shoulders or back.

"Actually, Mister Killiam, they are over-the-counter now. How often do you use them?" she inquired.

"Oh, man, I was a cigarette fiend. I have to use them everyday or I'll just go back to smoking," he replied. He reached for his blue shirt and thanked Pam for her attention as he gingerly put his arm through the right sleeve.

"I see. Did Pam remove it when she dressed your scrape?" Elise asked.

"Nah, here it is." Mr. Killiam twisted his body and pointed, to show the incredulous doctor. "I just slap it on before I go down for breakfast and I'm good all day!"

On his right shoulder, just below the soiled torn area where he had landed on the tarmac, was a square beige patch with the brand name and dosage imprinted on it.

Elise could barely stifle a laugh as she hurried out of the room. Should she ruin the placebo effect by telling Mr. Killiam that the nicotine is only absorbed when applied directly to the skin, or should she let him keep wasting his money? She decided, *why mess with success?*


In Room Three, Elise noted Leslee helping an elderly gentleman undress and placing him on the cardiac monitor. He was having great difficulty breathing and the conscientious doctor went in to assist. She glanced at her watch and figured she could get the patient plugged in and stabilized by the time her replacement arrived.

Mr. Jackson was a sixty-one year old black man who suffered from emphysema. One and a half packs of cigarettes a day for over fifty years had taken its toll on his lungs and he now had to be on oxygen all the time. The change in weather, coupled with a slight cold, had caused total decompensation.

His wheezing was audible without a stethoscope. Elise asked as few questions as possible to avoid stressing her ill patient. His barrel chest heaved as he gasped for air. His lips and fingernails were blue-tinged. She auscultated his heart and lungs.

"Albuterol and atrovent by nebulizer, then oxygen by ventimask at thirty-one percent. Keep his pulse ox ninety-two percent or better. Let's give him Solumedrol one hundred twenty-five milligrams I.V. push. Since he's already on Theodur, please get a level and run his aminophylline drip at..." Elise appraised Mr. Jackson's weight and punched numbers into her credit card-sized calculator. "...twenty-five milligrams per hour. Please order his old records and admitting labs, E.K.G., and portable chest. We'll get a blood gas after the second breathing treatment if he hasn't shown significant improvement."

By the time he had his second treatment, Mr. Jackson had improved enough to comment, "You don't look old enough to be a doctor."

Elise was relieved that Mr. Jackson would not require intubation. It was not easy to wean a *COPD-er*, a patient suffering from chronic obstructive pulmonary disease, from a ventilator. Sometimes you saved a patient only to condemn him to finish out his days on the respirator.

"I assure you I'm older than I look," she replied with a smile. In fact, Elise had plans to spend her thirtieth birthday tomorrow with her best friend, Janice, and her brother, Don.

Elise added a supplemental note to Mr. Jackson's chart and asked Leslee to arrange a bed in the respiratory care unit for the night. She called the medical resident covering the RCU and Mr. Jackson's personal physician. She was pleased she didn't have to turn over his care to Dr. Alan Flatt. She hated loose ends and preferred handling cases from start to disposition.

"Hey, Elise, how was your shift?" Alan said as he passed her en route to the lounge. His umbrella trailed muddy water on the linoleum.

"Quite something!" she said. "But I am ready to hit the road. Is it bad out?"

"It's raining and pretty slick out."

Elise finished the chart she was working on and joined Alan in the lounge to recount her shift.

"Speaking of babies, did you hear about Laura Peebles?"

Elise wrinkled her brow questioningly. "No, what?"

"So she's sleeping in one Saturday morning and the phone rings. It's Trisha, you know, the secretary from St. E's. She says, 'Where are you?' And Laura replies that she's in bed with Carl, where she belongs. Trisha informs her that she belongs in the E.D. and she's late. So Laura quickly gets dressed, cursing herself for not reading the schedule right. No sooner does she get to the E.D. than a young woman is brought in in active labor. Laura delivers the baby and says to the new mom, 'It's a beautiful baby girl. You must be so happy.' The woman says, 'No, actually I am putting it up for adoption. Do you want it?' And Laura says, 'Why, yes, I would.' So she calls Carl up on the phone and asks him. Two days later they went home with the baby."

"That is the most unbelievable story I've ever heard!" Elise exclaimed. "But now I understand why I got an invitation to a baby shower. I thought it was for her new puppy! That could only happen to Laura."

"Doctor Flatt, could we see you in Room Two, please?" an insistent disembodied nurse voice called out from behind the curtain.

"So it begins. Drive home safely," Alan admonished.

Elise grabbed her coat and briefcase. She was going to have to make a run for it because her umbrella was, where else, in the car. As she walked down the corridor, the paramedics burst through the door with a young man in a cervical collar and a backboard with copious bloodstains.

"We didn't have time to call it in," the novice EMT-P said loudly. "He's bad... MVA right around the corner."

His voice trailed off as they were led into the trauma room and everyone mobilized. Elise thought, *rainy days are C-collar days.*

She called out farewell but no one was listening. The tired resident left the emergency department satisfied that, not only hadn't she lost anyone today, but she had actually saved a few.

# CHAPTER 4

The bright sunlight filtered through the blinds and roused Elise from slumber. When she had to sleep during the day before or after a graveyard shift, she would wear dark blinders and earplugs. However, she hated wasting a minute of a precious day off and welcomed the heralding of the new day.

Emergency medicine residents actually had it good. Surgical residents were lucky if they had any days off in a month. They often worked five days a week from 5:30 am to 8:00 p.m. and at least performed rounds on the weekend days. They would be on call overnight every third to fourth night depending on their program and whether any fellow resident was vacationing. EM residents worked eighteen to twenty-one shifts per month, eight to twelve hours long depending on where they were training. The shifts were distributed between days, p.m.s, nights, and various overlapping double-coverage shifts. The situation was going to be even better for Elise next month because she was starting her four-month stint as chief resident at C.G.H. She would have increased administrative and teaching responsibilities and fewer clinical shifts.

Dressed in a teal jogging outfit and wearing matching yellow wristbands and headband, Elise gave Fluffers a can of something perfectly nutritious and positively foul-smelling. She grabbed her housekeys and went for a brisk two and a quarter mile run. It was exhilarating to breathe in the cool October morning air. The leaves had already changed and were falling off the trees into crunchy disorganized piles in Lincoln Park. Lake Michigan was smooth as glass and looked beautiful in the sparkling sun. Elise nodded in greeting to passing joggers, bicyclists, and Rollerbladers. Her feet slapped the jogging track in an even rhythm and her heart pounded steadily. *I don't* feel *old,* she thought ruefully.. On the way home, she even stopped off along the exercise trail which flanked the path and did some sit-ups and pull-ups.

Feeling rejuvenated, Elise returned to her apartment on Lake Shore Drive. She emptied the dishwasher out of sheer necessity because she was out of drinking glasses. She filled one with calcium enriched orange juice and plopped down on the recliner to listen to her answering machine messages.

"Happy birthday to you, happy birthday to you, you're thirty and old now, but I'm older than you!" crooned her father.

"And many more!" chimed her stepmother.

Click.

"Hello, hello? Elise, dahlink? I hate these machines. Can you hear me? It's Grandma. I'm calling to wish you a happy birthday. Hello?" Grandma was not very modern; remote control for the TV, yes, microwave and answering machines, no.

Click.

"Hey, hey, girlfriend! We'll be by at six to pick you up. Have a nice day!" Janice, her best friend, said.

Click.


Elise hopped in the shower. She deep conditioned her hair and then mentally imaged all her stress exiting down the drain with the rinsed suds. The birthday girl dressed in a black shirt of the softest cotton and a comfortable jean skirt and sat at her kitchen table reviewing the mail from the past two days. People living normal lives couldn't understand what a resident's life could be like. You often would let laundry pile up, mail go unopened, phone messages remain unanswered, so you could squeeze in some precious sleep between shifts and conferences.

At noon, she hopped on the El and went to meet her sister, Shelly, at Stefanis. Shelly had a hot date that night and was very apologetic that she couldn't join the others for dinner. She hoped treating Elise to a birthday lunch would make up for her absence. Living in a two-bedroom condo on the Gold Coast, she was a trader and did quite well for herself. Although there was a family resemblance in their facial features, Shelly was five feet, six inches tall, had gray-blue eyes, and long, wavy, dirty-blonde hair. Elise was older by eighteen months and the sisters were very close.

The women shared their experiences of the past week. Shelly told Elise a neophyte trader for a rival company had screwed up to the tune of fifty-thousand dollars with a poorly timed, poorly executed nosepick. Elise wasn't entirely sure she believed her, but Shelly was an artful storyteller anyway.

In a playful attempt at one-upsmanship, Elise repeated a story she had heard, "So one of our interns, Will Mahoney, was engaged by a police officer to pronounce a couple of DOAs."

Emergency department physicians had the responsibility of verifying that the police or funeral home directors truly had a person who was 'dead-on-arrival' in the back of their wagon or hearse. The procedure was to check for breath sounds and listen for a heart beat. Then one would examine the pupils to see if they reacted to light and squeeze a body part hoping for a neurologic response. If none of these were present, the patient was declared dead.

Shelly interrupted, "Who was it?"

Elise and Shelly's older brother, Don, was one of Chicago's finest and the sisters knew many of his fellow officers. His chosen profession was somewhat of a sore point to their father, who felt Don was wasting his intelligence as a policeman. He had hoped his son would be a lawyer, but the sisters recognized that Don's temperament was better suited to be a cop.

In a display of sibling extra-sensory perception, Elise clarified, "The policeman? Will didn't know. Anyway, the cop was very disturbed because some woman had apparently miscarried or aborted in a park by a bench and just left the poor fetuses there on the ground. They wanted them pronounced and then they were going to surrender the fetuses to the medical examiner. They were still deciding what charges they could press against the woman, if they found her."

Elise sipped her wine and chewed some calamari.

"Will was horrified and went out to the wagon. As a nice Catholic boy, he said he was thinking to himself, 'How heartless! How could a woman do such a thing?!' He said his heart was pounding and his stomach was churning. The cop was shining his flashlight in the back so they could see and Will leaned over, thinking to himself, 'Where am I going to put my stethoscope to listen for heart tones?' He looked at the tiny bodies and his eyes misted momentarily. Then, in a few moments, after his eyes adjusted to the dim light, he noticed, 'Wait a minute. Those are whiskers and those are paws, and that's a tail!' They weren't human fetuses at all, they were kittens!"

Shelly and Elise laughed raucously as the other diners stared at them. They finished their delicious veal and pasta dishes and deferred on dessert. Elise figured she'd be picking up enough calories at dinner when she would feel truly entitled to something ice creamy and chocolatey.

Shelly handed Elise a present.

"Happy birthday!"

Elise took the colorfully wrapped box out of the gift bag and unwrapped it. Inside she found a beautiful antique pin and birthday card. She read the humorous card making fun of her advanced age and affixed the pin on her shirt. She hugged her sister and thanked her.

As they separated in front of the restaurant, Elise called out to Shelly, "Have a great date tonight. Hope he's the one!"

"Happy thirtieth! Say hi to Don for me." Shelly waved as she hailed a cab.

Elise puttered around the house most of the afternoon relaxing; however, she did treat herself to a manicure and pedicure at a neighborhood salon. At five-fifteen, she applied her makeup and slipped on a short emerald green dress to accentuate her eyes. She put Shelly's pin on the right side and inspected herself in the mirror.

*Not bad for an old spinster of thirty.* First she pragmatically picked a clump of Fluffers' hair off the dress and then indulged in one more five minute period of feeling sorry for herself. Then, as a true emergency physician, she then pulled herself together and then banished those negative thoughts for the rest of the evening.

Don rang the doorbell at six o'clock sharp. Elise was pleasantly surprised. Her brother was not known for his promptness. In fact,

Janice would often tell him their plans were for a half-hour earlier than they really were to ensure their being on time.

Don looked more like their mother, with his deep brown eyes and dark brown, really almost black, hair. He had inherited his height from their father, thank goodness, and stood six-foot-one. He was quite handsome and well built, lifting weights and keeping in shape for his strenuous job. Elise had matched him up with Janice six months ago, against her better judgement, and they were still hot and heavy.

He hugged and kissed her.

"You look pretty hot for a thirty year old sister," he remarked.

Elise jabbed him in affected protest.

"C'mon, you know you're my favorite older, younger sister," Don pleaded.

"Let's go. Janice is out in the car waiting. The parking in your neighborhood stinks."

They drove to Elise's favorite Japanese restaurant, Sai Café, and had a wonderful meal. Elise couldn't bring herself to eat truly raw fish so she stuck to more benign California rolls with low sodium soy sauce. She ordered salmon teriyaki as her main dish. Don drank *sake* while Elise and Janice sipped plum wine.

Janice Goldberg was a tall, attractive woman with a curvy figure, a contagious laugh, and a fantastic sense of humor. She had curly black hair and cool blue eyes. She was a third year family practice resident who had met Elise in their internship year. The women had done their surgical rotation together and kept each other sane under crazy circumstances. They became instant and very close friends. Their relationship had greatly improved Elise's relationship with her brother.

At the conclusion of the meal, Janice confessed she had forgotten Elise's present at her place. "Come up so I can give it to you. It's still early, would you like to watch a movie?"

Elise tried begging off, but her companions would not hear of it. So they drove back to Janice's and, after two circles around the block, Don parked in a space about three inches longer than his impeccably maintained Mitsubishi Eclipse. Elise shuddered and had to close her eyes while he maneuvered.

Chatting loudly, they entered Janice's dark apartment and, as she flipped on the lights, everyone shouted, "Surprise!"

Elise was stunned. She felt like a deer caught in headlights; she wanted to turn and run, but she was paralyzed into inaction.

"Where is your date?" Elise accusatorily asked her sister who led the pack.

"That was an excuse - somebody had to get everything together here and let people in. Nice pin," she said with a grin, as she pointed out the expensive piece of jewelry she had given Elise earlier.

"I am overwhelmed," Elise said.

Don announced, "Ladies and gentlemen, we waited thirty years for this momentous occasion - my sister is...speechless!"

Everyone laughed. Elise was never at a loss for words.

She soaked it all in. Kathy and Carl were talking to several other nurses clustered around the vegetable tray and onion dip. Most of her fellow residents who had the night off were present, as were some of Don's and Shelly's friends who had become her friends, too. There were several paramedics clustered in a corner, drinking beers. They waved hello and lifted their glasses in a silent toast when they noticed her gaze.

The birthday celebrant smiled when she saw Al Flatt talking to Ann, a buxom nurse who did some professional singing on the side. He was quite the ladies' man and had a penchant for blondes. She then walked over to a handsome man standing by the table on which lay the sumptuous food spread.

"Mark, it's great to see you! How are your patients doing?"

"Still dead," he quipped.

Elise had taken a year off between medical school and residency. She spent the year working in the medical examiner's office assisting on autopsies. Mark Procino, M.D. was a young pathologist with whom she had worked. His smooth olive skin made a striking backdrop for his shining white teeth, a poster child for orthodontia. He had soulful brown eyes and a mop of thick, unruly, black hair that often fell over his right eye. They dated for a summer but eventually discovered they were better suited as friends. He smelled much better at night, of Drakkar Noir, than he did during the day, Elise recalled. She involuntarily wrinkled her nose.

They caught up for a while and Elise introduced him to some of the others. Elise mingled and swapped tales. Fortunately, there was enough variety in Elise's friends that conversation did not consist solely of medical stories. It was a source of major frustration to Elise that physicians had an annoying tendency to talk shop at social events. She had never realized how disconcerting it was for the layperson, until she attended an attorneys' function.

A group of lawyers were standing around and one was telling a joke. Elise listened avidly, but wasn't quite connecting. The story swelled to the climax, and the lawyer gave the punchline, "And he wanted a change of venue!" The rest of the crowd laughed uproariously and Elise shook her head, completely missing the joke. *This must be what we sound like to everyone else when we talk medicine*, she realized and vowed to try to never exclude anyone from the conversation again.

"Randy, how are you? Thanks so much for coming!" Elise greeted another resident in her year. The senior residents hardly ever got to work with one another because their shifts did not overlap. Except for conferences and social events, it was easy to lose touch with your peers.

"Happy birthday!" Randy said and kissed Elise on the cheek. "I'm doing pretty well. Leta and I are starting to look around. I'm planning on doing a toxicology fellowship and Leta is going to keep me in the style to which I would like to become accustomed."

Elise laughed. Leta, Randy and Elise had all started residency at the same time. Love bloomed and the two residents had married the previous June. Unfortunately, they had to postpone their honeymoon until September, because they had trouble coordinating their vacation schedule.

"How about you? Any ideas on what you are going to do next year?" Randy asked as Leta joined them and hooked her arm through his.

"I'm going to stay in the Chicago area. Some of the places I moonlight at may have openings, but I think I may stay at C.G.H. so I can stay involved with the residency program," Elise told them.

The low point of the night was the cake. Shelly delighted in pointing out that there wasn't enough room for all the candles on the ice cream sheet cake so she had placed a big "3" and "0" candle. It had almost slipped Elise's mind why everyone was gathered there.

"What a wonderful time! Thank you so much, I love you guys!" Elise gushed to her siblings and Janice as they cleaned up afterwards.

"I do throw great parties, don't I?" said the attractive trader with a satisfied look on her face.

And not to be outdone, Don quoted the old commercial, "And I helped!"

# CHAPTER 5

It was two-thirty a.m. Thursday morning and Elise was waiting for the drunk in Room Seven to either sober up or pass out. She didn't particularly care which avenue he took, as long as he was ultimately cooperative for his stitches. She also figured the longer it took, the less his breath would reek of cheap wine and cigarettes.

Elise whiled away the time by preparing for her Friday morning conference for the following week. She had spent almost a full month creating a database of interesting X-rays. Up until then, there were hundreds of handwritten lists through which the chief resident would manually pore to find examples of whatever subject he or she was planning to discuss. Elise had entered the patients' names, pathology, date of service, and medical record number. She then classified the radiograph according to type, such as chest x-ray, hand, pelvis, etc. The final category was the type of abnormality, such as fracture, dislocation, or tumor. The power of her new system was that one could quickly sort and obtain a set of a particular type of film, such as upper extremity fractures. It was easy to then pull the films, put together a handout and, *voilà*, Friday morning conference!

Several days previously she had used her new computer program to compile a list of C.T. scans of brains and she was now narrowing it down to several samples of each type of pathology to submit to the department of Radiology. When they gave her the films, she would look them over and select representative examples of different types of bleeds, tumors, and other lesions. Dr. Kaplan, the neuroradiologist, was going to be her guest instructor.

She was just finishing her list when Carmen Vargas, R.N., a stocky Mexican nurse who had long since eliminated all vestiges of an accent, interrupted her in the lounge.

"Elise, triage just brought back a kid having trouble breathing into Room Ten. Registration is making up the chart now."

"Thanks, I'll be right there," Elise said as she filed away her papers in her briefcase. She stood up and straightened out her lab coat over her scrubs. *Asthma season*, she thought as she walked between the rooms to reach Room Ten.

The minute she opened the door and surveyed the situation, she realized her guess had widely missed the mark. There was an approximately three year old boy sitting on his mother's lap in polka-dot feetsy pajamas. He had matted-down brown hair, apprehensive dark brown eyes, and his cheeks were flushed with fever. His chin jutted out past his chest and he appeared to be leaning forward, secured by his mother's loving arms. His mouth was slightly open and his tongue, pink but dry, was visible. Elise could hear a whistling sound, called stridor, as he inhaled. Elise took a step back out the door and waved to the nurse to approach her.

"Carmen, tell Bertha to call Radiology for the STAT-est portable soft tissue neck films they can muster up. Tell her to call Peds down and to get ENT on the phone for me. And get Doctor Weinfeld in here - we've got an epiglottitis," Elise rattled off quietly and calmly.

Elise had recognized the classic "sniffing position" from across the room, a position children with this disease assumed naturally to maximize the amount of air they could get into their systems. The epiglottis is a small triangular piece of tissue whose purpose is to protect the airway from substances "going down the wrong tube" when one swallows. Epiglottitis is an infection which causes this tissue to greatly swell and it can then block off the air passages and cause suffocation. In fact, the last thing doctors want to do is to agitate the child because that could trigger the catastrophe. So they do minimal handling and testing to diagnose the disease. The treatment is to have an ear-nose-and-throat specialist or an anesthesiologist place a tube in the child's windpipe in the operating room and then treat the infection with antibiotics until the swelling dissipates and the tube can be removed.

Elise checked the breast pocket of her lab coat and reassuringly patted the fourteen gauge I.V. angiocatheter which she always carried. If the airway blocked off precipitously, it was possible that she would be unable to intubate orally as was done under normal circumstances. In that case, she would need to create a temporary passage for the air to enter the lungs. That could be done by inserting the needle into the windpipe through the skin in the front of the neck and forcing air in with high pressure. Hopefully this would not become necessary, because the swollen epiglottis might prevent the expired air from exiting the body and that, too, would be dangerous.

"Elise, baby, I got ENT on the line," called out Bertha, the very large, very sweet, night clerk from Alabama. "Where do you want it?"

"-three-five," answered Elise, giving the terminal digits of the closest phone extension. The pediatric resident arrived at that moment, wiping the sleep from her eyes, and eavesdropped.

A masculine voice confronted her after she identified herself.

"What have you got?" he asked brusquely.

"I have an epiglottitis here. How fast can you get here?" ENT took call from home.

"Hold your horses. What did the soft tissues of the neck show?" he interrogated.

"X-ray is on its way..."

"You called me before you got the films back?!" he asked argumentatively.

Elise lost her cool. A child's life was at stake and she didn't give a hoot about the consultant's inflated ego. "Doctor Bartholomew, I have a three year old child with stridor trying desperately to breathe in my emergency department. The housekeeper could diagnose him with epiglottitis from across the room! I actually only ordered films because I know it will take you a little time to get in here - their only utility will be to complement my teaching file. Now, are you going to drag your sorry self in here, or should I call your attending directly and you can hear all about it tomorrow in morning report?"

"What year are you?" inquired the ENT resident arrogantly.

Dr. Weinfeld had sidled up alongside of her and sized up the situation. He was mouthing, "Do you want me to talk to him?" Elise shook her head in the negative.

"I'm the chief resident of emergency medicine and I'm looking forward to meeting you, too. Can I expect you in fifteen minutes?" she said in dulcet tones.

"Yes, I'll be there as quickly as I can," he said in a conciliatory attempt and then hung up.

"I'll let the O.R. staff know," offered Dr. Weinfeld and he set off to make the calls.

Dana Rubin, M.D., the peds resident who had heard Elise's half of the exchange, peered into Room Ten through the blinds which were adjusted accordingly. She returned to Elise and rolled her eyes.

"Looks like epiglottitis to me!" she said agreeably.

"We're lucky we can recognize it! I've only read about it. We hardly see any cases anymore now, thanks to the Hib vaccine," Elise acknowledged.

Elise removed her catheter and put it in her scrub shirt pocket. She removed her lab coat and suggested that Dana do the same. The less threatened the child felt, the less likely they were to set off further respiratory compromise. They entered the room quietly and stood near the door, allowing the child and mother to acknowledge them.

"Missus Koslowski, I'm Doctor Silver and this is Doctor Rubin from Pediatrics," Elise started. The chart had finally been processed and compiled, and she noted the child's name was John Koslowski and he was thirty-eight months old.

"What has taken so long?! My baby, he is sick!" screeched the panicked woman with a distinctly eastern European accent. The child looked agitated at his mother's distress.

"Ma'am, I'm sorry it has seemed like no one has been paying attention to your child, but let me explain. I took one look at John from the doorway and I recognized the severity of his illness. We believe he has something called epiglottitis..." and Elise went on to explain the condition to her. Elise gave her the details of what they needed to do and said, "Is Johnny up to date in his shots?"

"We have just come to America. He see doctor in two week for to check up," Mrs. Koslowski explained.

"Okay, the most important thing you can do now is be calm and keep Johnny relaxed. Is there anyone here with you, or someone you would like to call?"

Appeased, Mrs. Koslowski smoothed her only child's hair and murmured in her native tongue in his ear. The residents could see him relax slightly, although he was still obviously apprehensive.

"His father, I suppose," she answered softly.

"I'll have the nurse bring in the phone and she'll stay with you."

"I'll stay, too," Dana said as she dragged a stool over to the corner by the sink in the hope that Johnny would find her sufficiently unobtrusive.

Elise left the room relieved that Dana would sit vigil until the ear, nose, and throat specialist could arrive. As she was surveying the patient flow board, noting that Dr. Weinfeld had picked up several patients who had arrived in the interim, Dr. Bartholomew blew in. His body language said, "Boy, you'd better be right or there'll be hell to pay!"

Only minutes later, he was all business preparing a surgical consent for mom to sign in order to take the child to the O.R. Suffice it to say an apology was more than Elise could hope for, but as long as Johnny was getting the appropriate care, that was all the satisfaction Elise could need.


The next case on the flow board read, '*Crying.*' Elise picked up the chart and noted it was an eight-week-old infant. Her heart beat a little faster because a very ill baby could present with very few signs and could deteriorate without much warning.

The nurses had placed the tiny girl in Room Nine, and Elise could hear her shrieky squalling through the closed door. After an abbreviated evaluation, Elise was so concerned at how inconsolable the child was, she felt a septic work-up to check for a hidden infection was indicated. Elise was very worried because the baby kept drawing her legs up as though her abdomen hurt. Elise marked off the appropriate boxes on the order sheet and dropped it off at the clerk's desk as she collected the equipment to draw blood. She mentioned the case to Dana who promised to be in as soon as everything was squared away with John Koslowski.

As the doctor set up the tubes and needles to obtain the blood specimens, Bertha left her desk and walked into the Cast Room. She wheeled the cast cutter, a noisy loud contraption used to remove plaster casts, into Room Nine. Elise looked questioningly at her as it was highly unusual for big Bertha to venture out from behind her desk and unheard of for a clerk to enter a patient's room.

Bertha plugged in the device and flipped the switch on. The little infant stopped crying instantaneously and her eyes widened. The tension visibly melted away from her previously flailing little arms and legs. The mother looked just as startled as her offspring and Elise was the most surprised in the crowd.

"Doc, the Good Lord blessed me with twelve young'uns and two of 'em had the colic. If that ain't the hollerin' of colic, tie me up like a pig, shove an apple in ma mouth, and stick me on a spit," she shouted over the loud drone of the machine. With that, she proudly wheeled her bulky body around and exited the room.

Elise look bewildered and turned to Dana who had just slipped in the room.

"I don't get it. Isn't she too old for colic to start?"

Dana shrugged and asked, "How old is your little girl, ma'am?"

The mother responded, "Eight weeks old."

Dana looked slightly puzzled and starting telling Elise how colic usually begins at approximately two to four weeks old and there are stringent criteria for calling extreme fussiness "colic" when the mother interrupted.

"Well, Katie's eight weeks old but she came a month and a half early."

Dana and Elise both shook their heads in understanding. Premature babies develop according to their gestational age, most easily calculated by using their due date. Katie was actually like a two week old baby and early colic was now a much more likely diagnosis. The doctors would have to rule out more serious illness and her pediatrician would have to watch how the symptoms progressed, but Bertha would ultimately turn out to be right after all.

Dr. Weinfeld and Elise met at the patient flow board and assessed the condition of the department. There were still eight patients in rooms, and two yet to be seen.

"*Abdominal pain* and *boil on the butt*. I'll toss you for it," Dr. Weinfeld said.

Elise remembered the last incision and drainage she had done. Despite four milligrams of Versed and eight of morphine, the patient howled during the entire procedure. About ten cc. of the thickest, grossest smelling pus Elise had ever seen came oozing out. In fact, a tuna and swiss cheese hero with red onion on it, left forgotten on the front seat of a black minivan parked in the outdoor long term parking lot at Midway airport for a week in midsummer, would smell like Chanel No. 5 by comparison. At the time, it made even the veteran emergency medicine resident feel faint. Actually, just recalling the incident made her want to retch all over again.

"Oh, no, Rob, I think abdominal pain is much more of a teaching case. You can take the perirectal abscess!" Elise replied. And before her attending had a chance to argue, Elise had the chart in her hand and was en route to Room Six.

"Miss Amaguchi, I'm Doctor Silver. What seems to be the problem tonight?" Elise began her questioning.

"I'm having terrible stomach cramps," replied the patient.

Ms. Amaguchi was a forty-two year old Amerasian woman, lying on the cart, curled up in a fetal position. Her abdomen looked distended and she grimaced regularly.

Elise quickly collected the information she needed. The abdominal pain had been progressive since approximately ten o'clock at night. Nausea, vomiting, and a low grade fever had accompanied the pain. Ms. Amaguchi had only had a vaginal hysterectomy in the past, and still owned a gallbladder and appendix. She had never had similar pain before, even with her babies. Her last bowel movement had been a day ago and was rather hard, but no blood had been sighted.

The physical examination suggested something serious going on in the woman's abdomen. It was bloated and the bowel sounds were abnormal. When Elise tapped on her belly to size her liver, Ms. Amaguchi moaned because the right part of her lower abdomen hurt. She was extremely tender there when Elise directly pressed, and even when she released.

Elise ordered laboratory tests, urine tests, x-rays, and intravenous fluids. She noted '*NPO*' on the chart indicating that Ms. Amaguchi was not to eat or drink anything until Elise allowed her to. Finally, she reported to the surgical intern her findings and cheerfully requested he come down and evaluate the patient.


"Mister Parker is bellowing for you. By the way, his alcohol level is on his chart," said Kenny, the orderly.

He followed Elise into the room where the soused patient lay fully restrained in wide leather straps on a cart. They were disgusted to note that the drunken man had freed up one hand just enough to unzip his fly. He had impeccable aim and had created a swathe of unsterility from the foot of his cart to the bandages on the countertop by way of the footstool parked aside his gurney. To prevent a repeat occurrence, Kenny none too gently placed a Texas catheter, which is like a condom attached to a tube emptying into a bag, on Mr. Parker's penis. Kenny then grabbed a mop and pail of disinfectant, and Elise gathered her suture material and set them up on the bedside table.

"I know my rightsh," Mr. Parker slurred. "You can't sew me up unless I let you. And I don't!"

"Mister Parker, you are misinformed," Elise wearily explained. "I am obliged by the Hippocratic oath to treat you appropriately, whether you like it or not, and whether I like *you* or not. Tomorrow when you are sober, you could sue me for *not* sewing you up. However, no jury would award you a penny for my sewing up a laceration as nasty as that, even if it was against your will."

"Hey, I know my rightsh!" he perseverated. "Who the fuck do you think you are?!"

Elise was fed up. It was four-thirty in the morning and she was hitting the wall. She couldn't stomach the sickening sweet smell of blood mixed with old booze and Mr. Parker was grating on her last nerve. She leaned over and calmly explained the situation to the inebriated man.

"Who the fuck do I think I am? I am the physician who is about to stitch up the huge, deep gash on your head whether you like it or not and I can either use numbing medicine, or not! Now, are you going to be a good boy and cooperate, or does Kenny need to hold you down? Frankly, I couldn't care less which way we do this," she finished crossly.

Sullenly, Mr. Parker stopped straining and lay back on the cart. Beads of sweat accented his weather-beaten forehead. Elise examined the area Kenny had already shaved and prepared with antiseptic. She shook her head in disbelief. About three inches to the left of the fresh scalp cut was an older previously treated laceration, and its stitches were deeply embedded and encrusted with dried blood and dirt. Mr. Parker obviously had disregarded a follow-up appointment to have his last set of sutures removed. *Oh well*, Elise thought, *I'll kill two birds with one stone.* She meticulously stitched up the new laceration with sutures which would be absorbed. It was not standard practice, and would leave a nastier scar. But she figured that it was on his scalp in his hair, and her keen powers of deduction suggested to her that he was unlikely to be holding down a modeling job by day. Besides, this way he wouldn't need a follow-up visit to a medical health care provider which he would blow off. The weary resident then painstakingly picked out the crusty old stitches.

Mr. Parker was making a racket snoring when Elise left his room. She stretched and twisted trying to work the kinks out in her back as she dictated a procedure note documenting what she had done. She vowed one day that she would remember to adjust the height of the gurney so she wouldn't ache after sewing. Elise walked over to Bertha's desk where the night staff was congregating during the early morning lull.

"Where's the list?" Elise asked as she flourished the computer printout with the lab result.

"I gots it," wheezed Bertha.

"And the ETOH level is..." She paused for the dramatic effect. One dollar and fifty cents was riding on who guessed the closest to

Mr. Parker's alcohol level without going over. He was slurring his speech and wobbly on his feet, his eyes showed nystagmus. The fly in the ointment, however, was Mr. Parker was a chronic alcoholic so his system was likely to be able to tolerate a higher level with the same symptoms.

"Four fifty-six!" Elise read aloud. *If I had that level, I would probably be comatose or dead!*

Bertha scanned the list.

"Dang! Doc Weinfeld, you won agin! He guest four hunnerd twenty-two. I thinks you must cheat," she accused as she turned over the booty.

He laughed.

"That's why they pay *me* the big bucks, Bertha."

As per usual, Dr. Weinfeld deposited the money in the makeshift coffee-can bank for the coffee fund located in the lounge.

"I'm going to Xrayland to check on Miss Amaguchi's films, everyone," Elise called out.

Minutes later, as the radiology resident and Elise pored over the odd abdominal series, the surgical intern came storming into the reading room.

"Shit, shit, shit!" he exclaimed.

Elise glanced at him disparagingly for the use of such profane language. "What is your problem?"

"What did you find on rectal exam?!" he challenged angrily.

Elise sweetly explained that since she was certain a surgical consultation was indicated, she wanted to save the patient having to go through multiple rectal examinations. She, therefore, had deferred that part of the physical to him.

"Don't do me any fucking favors next time!" he rudely growled.

Elise abruptly turned her attention away from him and asked Dave Relkey, the radiology resident, what his preliminary interpretation of the films was.

"It's weird looking, Elise. There's free air, but it also looks like an obstruction and the stool pattern is just plain funky," he reported.

The surgical intern interjected roughly, "Kind of like what about a billion pumpkin seeds would look like all conglomerated in a colon?"

Elise gave him a double take and he continued, "If you had done a rectal, maybe you would have been stuck instead of me. This lady has been eating pumpkin seeds for weeks and she eats them shell and all. Well, they're freaking sharp and I cut my index finger right through my damn glove!"

"I'm going to guess that they have also torn a hole in her intestine as well," offered the senior emergency medicine resident. "Did you get cleaned up?"

"What do you think?" he answered sarcastically.

"I think we are going to need to draw bloods on Miss Amaguchi and you. You're going to need to undergo the needlestick protocol. I can't be sure, but I tend to doubt that she's likely to be H.I.V. positive," Elise tried to reassure him.

"All I can say is I better get to scrub in on *this* one!" the resident avowed loudly as they walked back to the E.D.. "And I don't mean just holding the stupid retractors!"

Elise packaged Ms. Amaguchi for surgery and admission and rechecked her drunk in Room Seven. He was beginning to be a little penitent for his awful behavior earlier. The compassionate and forgiving resident responded by removing two of his restraints.

Elise went into the lounge to collect her briefcase and down coat and found Dr. Weinfeld sitting on the couch with his eyes closed. She folded her stethoscope and put it in the pocket of her lab coat. She then placed her coat on the hook behind the lounge door.

"I'm only leaving Mister Parker in Room Seven. He seems to be improving appropriately so I held off on a C.T. scan. I've documented his laceration repair and several repeat exams. There were no focal neurological findings. Did ENT call down on that kid, by the way?"

Dr. Weinfeld softly chuckled.

"Yeah. He specifically asked for me. I think he was too gutless to tell you you were right. You did a good job tonight, Elise," he praised.

"Thanks, Rob. Good night," Elise answered.

"Drive safely. Have security walk you to your car."

Elise walked out of the lounge and called out, "Good night, everybody! See you next time."

# CHAPTER 6

*That's a nice subtle chronic subdural hematoma*, she thought as she held up a C.T. film to the viewbox and saw a small amount of fluid in the temporoparietal area. She placed it in her "to use" set as she compiled the films she planned to use in her conference.

*I don't even see this sinusitis, wonder what the official report said?* The E.D. doctors entered the cases on the interesting x-ray list and sometimes their preliminary readings did not jive with the official radiology interpretations. Elise replaced the films in the folder and put it on the reject pile.

*That's funny, this huge bleed looks just like that other one I already picked out. The hemorrhage is kind of shaped like Africa*, she marveled. Elise sifted through her stack of positives until she found the other case of massive intracranial hemorrhage involving the ventricles, with herniation. She carefully compared the films, puzzled. Finally, she superimposed one atop the other on the illuminated view box. Besides the names and dates, the radiographs were identical down to every curve and indentation of the brain matter. *That's impossible*, Elise thought, *that would be like two sets of identical fingerprints.*

She copied down the names of the patients. The first patient, John Babcock, Jr., had predated her arrival to C.G.H., but the second, Jefferey Morris Weber, birth date: January 15, 1919, date seen: August 24, 2000, sounded vaguely familiar to her.

A subarachnoid hemorrhage, brainstem tumor, and acoustic neuroma capped off her collection and Elise walked the rejects back to Radiology. She stopped off at Medical Records to request Mr. Weber and Mr. Babcock's charts and went to the third floor to the library to put together a handout on how to interpret computerized tomography of the skull and brain.

At noon, Elise grabbed a chicken filet sandwich, fries and a Pepsi and went to the hospital auditorium. She saw her friend, Janice, and made her way down the row to sit next to her. The place was packed and people continued to stream in. Everyone was anxious to hear what Dr. Shulman had to say.

"Good afternoon, everyone. I would like to thank you all for attending. As you know, here at Chicago General Hospital, we feel like a great big family. Sometimes, when there are important matters, you have to have a family meeting. That is how I view this forum. I would like to give you some information and I will be happy to take questions at the end," Dr. Shulman said in introduction.

Elise thought to herself that Dr. Shulman was an accomplished speaker. *He sounds so sincere, like he really does care about each and every one of us.*

"Historically, doctors and hospitals worked on a fee-for-service basis. This meant we did tests or treatments which we hopefully felt were necessary, and then submitted bills with our charges. The insurance companies would then pay us some percentage of our charges, often relative to the other hospital charges in the area. There were several consequences of this system in this imperfect world. Some unscrupulous people probably abused this system and did nonessential things to drive up charges. In the same vein, some providers raised charges to try to increase what they were paid. Lastly, excessive tests were performed out of fear of malpractice. However, I would like to think here at C.G.H. we have always tried to be cost effective while providing top notch medical care to our patients."

"I hate ordering stupid things because we are at such high risk to be sued. Like x-raying every whiplash even though I know their necks are not broken. And the workmen's comp!" Elise complained in a whisper.

"Then came the concept of getting paid a set amount for each enrolled patient. When do you think this was first tried?"

Dr. Shulman waited patiently as a few half-hearted responses were shouted out. He smiled and continued.

"It was in the year, nineteen-ten, out in California. I can't recall whether it was a logging or railroad company, but they set up a contract where they were paid fifty cents per member per month. Of course, in those days, the technology consisted of leeches and snake oil, so they probably made out okay.

"Doctor Kaiser and Doctor Garfield started their managed care organization in nineteen-thirty-three and slowly other cooperatives developed. In the nineteen-seventies, the movement gained further momentum, but was still not in the mainstream.

"But then came the attempt at health care reform. Even though it failed, Clinton's movement caused major repercussions in the system. These health maintenance organizations, or H.M.O.s, which were already in existence, started gaining popularity. And that is why we are talking today.

"The basis of payment in an H.M.O. is called 'capitation'. This means that a doctor is paid a set amount for each enrollee. If John Doe is very healthy and safe, Doctor X, and the H.M.O., come out ahead. If John requires a lot of testing or treatment, Doctor X's profit dwindles and can disappear. Why does the doctor submit to this? Pretty much because they have been forced to. Because the H.M.O. has low fees, companies select it to provide their employees with health insurance. And the H.M.O. limits the physicians the patient may choose as his health care provider. So, the doctor either joins the H.M.O. and complies, or ends up out of business.

"What are the consequences of such a system? Sometimes physicians are inclined to cut corners to save money. They opt for watching a patient over a period of time instead of ordering a C.T. scan which costs hundreds of dollars. They prescribe an antibiotic for a chronic cough instead of getting a chest x-ray which might show the patient's early lung cancer. You could well imagine this might affect the quality of care provided to patients.

"Now, hospitals have a slightly different problem. There are several different approaches for an H.M.O. Sometimes the H.M.O. contracts with a hospital, paying a set amount per patient. There is then a tendency for the individual physicians to overuse resources, like laboratory and radiology studies because they are not responsible for payment. This ends up jeopardizing the hospital's financial stability. The institution has little control over costs like technology, electricity, and supplies. Now, it essentially has no control over charges because there is a fixed payment set-up. So if too many unnecessary carotid duplex studies are performed, the hospital is the big loser.

"Another method is for the H.M.O. to buy up hospitals in a region. They can close down facilities if they don't like their bottom line. They can arrange for specific hospitals to specialize in certain medical problems. This serves to increase the volume of a given disease process at an individual facility. The flip side is that their other institutions don't incur the overhead expenses to care for that type of patient. This can be an inconvenience to the patients and their families, because each service is not locally available to them. They may need to drive into the next town for obstetric services or for the burn center.

"This is the issue that is striking us hard, here at C.G.H. Medcare Healthnet is a health maintenance organization which originated in southern California. It is rapidly working its way eastward. They have recently snatched up three smaller hospitals here in the Chicagoland area, one just down the street from us. They are negotiating to form a consortium with several others, but, of course, Medcare is forcing everyone to severely discount their services.

"Why are insurance companies moving in this direction? Obviously because it favors them financially. Even Medicaid, which never had marvelous reimbursement to begin with, is undergoing a massive shift towards H.M.O.s. Again, why do patients buy into this system? Because they have no choice! If you work at Metro Toyota and their health plan is Medcare Healthnet, you must go to Medcare Healthnet providers and hospitals.

"This is another major problem for us. There are complex regulations stipulated by H.M.O.s which patients are expected to abide by. However, it is easy for the H.M.O. to say at the outset, 'You have to call your doctor to obtain permission to be seen in the emergency department.' It is entirely another thing to force patients to comply.

"So patients show up at our doorstep, a non-participating hospital, requesting medical attention. There are strict governmental regulations mandating us to do at least a medical screening, regardless of ability to pay. Thankfully, the government has tried to institute the 'prudent layperson' rule. This essentially states that if the average person would think he had an emergency, such as pain, dysfunction, or blood coming from someplace it doesn't usually come from," a smattering of giggles was heard, "the visit should be considered a valid emergency visit. Despite this 'prudent layperson' definition, if the H.M.O. determines retrospectively that the reason the patient went to the emergency department is actually a non-emergent problem, they are likely to resist paying for our services. If the H.M.O. demands we transfer a patient whom we thought was stable, but they deteriorate en route or have a bad outcome, we are the ones who are held solely liable. H.M.O.s have devised a tricky way of avoiding any medicolegal or financial responsibility in these cases.

"Okay, what exactly does all this mean to me, you must be wondering. If Chicago General Hospital wants to survive in this environment, we are going to need to make some drastic changes. We need to make our services attractive to employers and other third party payers. What do they care about? Money. So we have to make sure our charges are competitive. How can we do it? We need to lower our costs."

A disgruntled murmur ran through the audience. The battle cry to lower costs had been heard before, and it was never good news.

"'How so?', I hear you all asking. Well, there are many facets to our money saving plan. Starting today, each department is expected to put together a taskforce consisting of personnel from every level. Their common goal is to evaluate the current operations and figure out how to provide the same level of excellent care less expensively. We need to minimize waste everywhere. I expect a preliminary report in two weeks. The message I want to convey to you all today is, 'Every band-aid helps!'

"The administration has already made some recommendations. We believe that it will be more cost effective to cross-train personnel to perform multiple tasks like blood drawing, E.K.G.s, inserting I.V.s, and stocking the rooms. Scheduling clerks are going to be cross-trained as registrars to ensure we know which patients need pre-authorization for the H.M.O.s with which we do business currently. There will be a shift in our physician mix toward general practitioners, not excessive sub-specialists, much as is being seen across the nation. We are hoping this will not result in massive lay-offs, but we are not likely to be hiring new ancillary personnel in the near future."

More grumbling was heard in the audience.

"Yeah, I spend most of my day with my feet up, just waiting for a nurse to find something for me to do," a stocky orderly, sitting two rows ahead of Elise, said loudly and sarcastically.

Dr. Shulman waited for the furor to die down. He continued, "We also have been looking seriously at the trauma designation. As you might imagine, patients with penetrating trauma, like gunshot wounds or stab wounds, are often underinsured or carry no insurance at all. This is a huge financial burden on our system, as these patients are often severely injured and have costly stays in the intensive care unit followed by lengthy recuperation and rehabilitation. We end up eating the cost of this care. Let me be clear, the board has had heated discussions regarding this. We know this is a need of our community, but, if we continue to provide trauma care, our hospital may not survive to provide any other type of care."

Elise inhaled sharply. *What would that do to the emergency medicine and surgical residencies? How would they learn how to manage trauma if their institution no longer was a trauma center? This did not bode well.* Elise had a fleeting thought that she was glad she wasn't irrevocably committed to staying at Chicago General yet. The future of C.G.H. was looking somewhat fragile, from what she could gather from Dr. Shulman's talk.

"Another concession we are making is the physician staff is foregoing its cost-of-living raises for the first three months of next year. Everyone is chipping in and tightening up his belt.

"In conclusion, I hope I have not sounded overly pessimistic. Chicago General Hospital is a venerated institution and we have a duty to our patients. We also feel strongly that we want our personnel to be secure and happy working here. We are going to need to make changes, some drastic, but I am convinced that if we all pitch in and help, C.G.H. will weather this storm, too. If any of you out there have suggestions, I implore you to become involved with your departmental task force and help us find the solutions to our problems.

"Thank you all for your time and attention. I will be happy to entertain questions now," Sid concluded.

There was a smattering of reluctant applause. Some people stood up to leave and Elise looked at her watch.

"I have to go. My shift starts at one," she whispered to Janice.

"I'm going to stay and listen to the questions. I'll let you know what they say," Janice promised. She was planning on staying on in the department of family medicine and was, naturally, very concerned as well.

"Give me a call in the E.D. after dinner. Say hi to Don for me," the emergency medicine resident said as she sidled out.

Dr. Shulman called on a middle-aged African American woman wearing pale green scrubs and a surgical cap sitting in the middle of the auditorium, first. Elise exited the side door as the woman stood and began posing her question.

"Well, that was pretty ugly," Elise said quietly to herself. She mused the implications of what Dr. Shulman had said as she strode to the E.D.


The resident entered the emergency department at the same time as the paramedics came through the door with an elderly black male. Elise set her briefcase down in the lounge and went into Room Three before the paramedics had finished transferring their charge onto the hospital gurney.

"Hey, Carlos, Dean. What have you got for me?" Elise asked amicably as she helped lift the patient over to the cart.

"Hey, Doc, how's it going?" Carlos responded, without actually waiting for an answer. "Mister Howell is in his seventies and his landlady found him unconscious on the floor near the phone. She said she heard a thud and, when he didn't answer her knocking, she used her spare key to let herself in. He supposedly lives with his daughter, but she wasn't there. We found a bottle of Micronase in the kitchen. His initial vital signs were BP, one-forty over seventy, pulse, sixty-two, and respirs of twenty-four."

"What have you done for him so far?" she inquired.

"We got him on the monitor and found him in sinus tach. I put him on four liters of oxygen by nasal cannula. We pitched him in the rig and I started a line of normal saline at a moderate rate. His glucose was forty so I gave him an amp of $D_{50}$. It was weird actually. He seemed to respond initially, but he lapsed back into unconsciousness," Carlos finished his presentation.

Elise turned her attention to Debby, the nurse with a pixie face and a talent for baking which she exercised regularly. She was in the process of removing Mr. Howell's clothes and wordlessly brought Elise's attention to the fact that the elderly patient had lost control of his bladder.

"Deb, can I have an accucheck, please? Let's get him on the monitor, and I want a twelve-lead. Send off the bloods that Carlos got for a C.B.C., comprehensive metabolic panel, PT/PTT, and let's get a gas," Elise instructed as she began a systematic examination of the patient. Although didn't find any signs of trauma, she did notice that he seemed malnourished. Mr. Howell had some coarse breath sounds at the bases, his otherwise his heart and abdomen were normal. A neurologic exam was not productive in his obtunded state.

Two minutes later, Debby informed her that Mr. Howell's sugar was 126.

"That's curious. I expected it to be low again. Could you give him one hundred milligrams of thiamine and then another amp of dextrose anyway?" Elise asked.

There was no response, so Elise mentally ran down her unconscious patient protocol. "Okay, please give him two milligrams of Narcan," she ordered.

No sooner was that pushed in than Mr. Howell began to rouse. He started flailing his arms and yelling in a slurred voice. He began trying to sit up and get off the cart.

"I need some help in here," Debby called out urgently into the department.

Several fellow nurses and the attending, Dr. Hewston, responded rapidly. Janet rushed out to grab soft restraints even as Elise tried to talk Mr. Howell down.

"Mister Howell, do you know where you are?" she asked.

He mumbled something unintelligible so Elise told him where he was. She asked if he knew why he was there.

"Does anything hurt?" she tried.

He was really not responding appropriately.

"Can I have some vitals, please?" Elise requested.

"Already on it, Elise," Stephanie answered. She was a nurse who normally worked nights but was doing a double shift today. "BP is two hundred over one-twenty-four, pulse is sixty-four, and respirations are twenty-four."

Elise quickly synopsized the case for Katriona.

She thought aloud, "At first I thought it was a straightforward case of hypoglycemic reaction to an oral diabetic agent, but it's more complex than that. Do you think his vital signs are reflective of a Cushing's response?"

Dr. Hewston expounded for the sake of those present, "Hmmm, his blood pressure is elevated and his heart rate is slow. That could be consistent with what you would see in the case of increased intracranial pressure. If he was twenty years old and a heroin addict, I'd think the Narcan had made him withdraw, though, the way he is acting."

"Maybe he had a bleed and that was what caused him to fall, and then his sugar dropped," speculated Debby.

"All I know is he bought himself a C.T. scan," Elise declared. "Guess I'm not going to use Labetalol on him."

Katriona giggled at Elise's joke. Since the patient's heart rate was already quite slow, Elise was going to have to select a blood pressure lowering medication that would not slow it further like that particular drug would.

"How about some Ativan to calm him down, instead?" suggested the staff physician.

Once that was done, the crisis was temporarily under control. Elise went out to the physician's charting area and dialed the radiologist's number.

"Hi, Sanjiv, I need a plain brain," Elise entreated. She told him the story and explained they wanted to rule out a brain hemorrhage.

"Have the clerk enter the order in the computer, and I'll let the techs know he's next," Sanjiv said agreeably.

Elise meticulously documented everything in the chart and instructed Debby to stay with the patient in C.T. scan. Debby placed Mr. Howell on a portable monitor so she could watch his rhythm. She wheeled his cart expertly out the automatic doors and left the E.D.

Elise's next patient didn't meet her eyes when she entered his cubicle. He was lying on the gurney, with his face averted towards the wall.

"Carter, how are you?" the resident cheerfully greeted the frequent flyer.

Carter Franklin was a twenty-seven year old black schizophrenic who came to the E.D. at Chicago General about twenty times per year. Interns cut their psychiatric eyeteeth on Carter. His modus operandi was to stop taking his anti-psychotic medication and then get rip-roaring drunk or stoned periodically. Then, he would freak out some unsuspecting passerby who would involve the police. The police all knew Carter intimately and he would find himself brought to C.G.H. to be admitted for a few weeks of drying out. Once out, he would start drinking alcohol and doing crack cocaine and stop taking his prescribed drugs again. The cycle would start over.

"So what brings you in today, Carter?" Elise prodded.

"They after me," he responded, his voice slightly slurred.

Elise thought that his answer, paranoid though it be, might actually be related to her question. She was impressed. Often his responses had no correlation whatsoever with what was being asked of him.

"Who's after you?"

"Don't throw nothing at it 'cause it breaks," was the non sequitur answer.

Elise had to laugh and jotted this down. Carter was such a pro at being evaluated, he was prematurely giving an interpretation, albeit a very literal one, of the proverb, "People who live in glass houses shouldn't throw stones."

"Carter, we're not up to the mental status examination yet! Please try to stay with me. Does anything hurt?" Elise redirected.

"Yeah, they gave me some bad stuff," he replied as he rubbed his upper abdomen. "Mine eyes have seen the glory of the coming of the Lord. Why are you so small?" Carter said as he blinked back tears staring fiercely at the doctor seated by the wall.

She wrote down a few more examples of his nonsensical conversation and then Elise approached him to examine him. He had already been stripped and placed in a gown. Security had thoroughly gone through his clothing to ensure there were no drugs or weapons. His clothes had then been bagged and placed elsewhere. Not that this would necessarily prevent a psychiatric patient from absconding from the E.D. It was not unheard of for a particularly motivated psychotic patient to slip out of the department in a hospital gown, complete with posterior ventilation and no undergarments, sans shoes, and be found walking down Michigan Avenue in the snow in late December.

She wrinkled her nose in distaste. Her patient smelled like a urinal in a distillery, with overlays of vomit. She donned gloves and rapidly examined him. She noticed he was somewhat dehydrated and his entire upper abdomen was tender. Fortunately she did not find any blood in his stool on rectal examination. He had some neurologic findings which suggested alcohol intoxication to Elise.

"Carter, we're going to need to do the usual tests," she informed him. The emergency physician's primary responsibility to the psychiatric patient was to ascertain that there was nothing medical going on with him or her. Psychiatric patients could become physically ill and it could be dangerous to ignore that and solely address the mental condition. Once the patient was 'medically cleared,' psychiatry could finish the patient's definitive treatment.

Elise found her attending to quickly review the case.

"Katriona, Carter Franklin is here."

Dr. Hewston rolled her eyes.

"Again? I think he was here just a few weeks ago," she answered. "Do the usual."

"I'm going to, but I think he may be sick today, too. He reeks of alcohol," Elise informed her superior who cut her off brusquely.

"Why should today be different? He's always drunk," she interrupted.

"Yeah, but he's having belly pain, too. I'm going to hydrate him with a yellow bag and make him NPO. I'll run liver enzymes, and check his amylase and lipase for pancreatitis. I think I'll also get an abdominal series," the resident finished.

"Okay, I'll go see him in a little bit," Katriona approved.

Elise also marked down routine labs, an alcohol level, and a drug screen. She ordered an intravenous to hydrate him up. When thiamine and vitamins were added to give the alcoholic much needed supplements, they would turn the I.V. fluids bright yellow. As she went to turn in the orders, Wanda caught her attention.


"Registration told me that Mister Howell's family is here. Do you want to talk to them?" the clerk said.

"Fantastic! Could you have them go into the Quiet Room? I'll be there in a jiffy," Elise answered.

As Wanda called out front and instructed the registrar to show the family to the Quiet Room, Elise set her chart into the appropriate box. She straightened her hair and buttoned her coat to conceal an errant splotch of Betadine. The resident picked up Mr. Howell's chart so she could document additional information and walked to the Quiet Room.

"Hello, I'm Doctor Silver. You are the family of Mister Howell?" Elise asked for confirmation.

"Yes. I'm his daughter and this is his niece. When I got home, his landlady told me he was here. I called Ella for a ride and we got here as soon as we could," a middle-aged woman in an ill-fitting plaid coat answered. Even across the room, Elise could hear her wheezing as she breathed. The doctor hoped that the woman wasn't going to end up as her next patient!

"Are you all right?" Elise asked in a concerned tone of voice.

"You mean Addie's breathin'? She always breathes like that. Don't pay her no mind," the niece interjected.

"Okay, well, if you need help, let us know. Now, can we talk about your father?" Elise asked.

"Yeah. How's he doing?" Addie asked.

"He's stable for the moment. It would help me greatly if you could answer some questions."

"I'll do my best," the woman promised.

"What kind of medical problems does your dad have?" Elise questioned.

"Sugar, and prostrate cancer. He also has high blood."

Elise's sharp mind was whirring. *Perhaps he had metastases to his brain and had experienced bleeding around one of the lesions. That might explain his condition.*

"What medications does he take?" she asked, pen poised to write the names down.

"I brought the bottles. I'm no good at them names," Addie admitted.

"You did great bringing them. May I see?" Elise asked excitedly.

She pawed through the brown paper bag. Micronase, for his diabetes, as the paramedics had mentioned. Tenormin, for blood pressure control. *Well, that explained his slow heart rate.* HCTZ, a water pill also for blood pressure. Another bottle of Tenormin, this one empty. MS-Contin and Tylenol with codeine, for pain.

Elise looked up sharply.

"Has your father's prostate cancer spread?" she asked as gently as she could.

His daughter answered, "He has it in his bones. He gets Lupron shots for that."

"Well, your dad should be coming back from brain scan soon. His blood sugar dropped too low from his diabetes medicine and we treated that. Then he started acting oddly so we took the precaution of making sure his brain was okay," Elise explained. "The nurse will come get you when he returns from radiology."

Elise strode back into the department just as Mr. Howell was being wheeled back. She checked on him and found him sleeping soundly again. His blood pressure had normalized again. She sought Dr. Hewston out.

"Katriona, guess what!"

"What?" Katriona answered.

"You know that old guy in Three, the one who you guessed would be a heroin addict if he was younger? How about if he was on morphine and codeine and we gave him Narcan? He'd have the same physiologic response of withdrawal. But imagine if he was on a beta-blocker. Even though normally his heart rate would speed up, the medication would prevent him from getting tachycardic. I think that explains Mister Howell. He's got metastatic prostate CA and is on MS-Contin and T-4s."

"Good case, Elise. Just check his C.T. and then get him admitted."

"If it's negative, I was thinking I'll admit him on observation status. I'll check with his oncologist first," Elise added.

"Sounds like a plan," Katriona said and walked over to the phone to talk an attending call.

Sue Joseph was the intern working the day shift. She had looked in on all the activity in Room Three earlier and had been standing nearby during the doctors' discussion of the case. She was a little puzzled.

"Why does he need to be admitted? Why can't you just feed him and send him out?" she asked.

"That's a good question, Sue," Elise said. "If Mister Howell were a diabetic who used insulin, that is exactly what we would do. But since the oral medication he takes is long lasting, he is at risk for having another hypoglycemic reaction. And this time he might not be so lucky. Every second that your blood sugar is too low, you run the risk of seizures, brain damage, and even death."

Elise walked over to radiology to look at the C.T. with Sanjiv. It showed atrophy, but no evidence of bleeding or tumor.

"Have you seen belly films on Franklin come by yet?" Elise asked the swarthy radiology resident.

Sanjiv flipped through a small stack in front of him. He picked out a folder and mounted the films on the view box. The two residents noted the suggestion of sluggish digestion, but there was nothing indicating a burst or blocked intestine.

"Ileus, and maybe a few calcifications around the pancreas. Is he a drinker?" Sanjiv asked. It was an occupational hazard that radiologists were often given no clinical information on the x-ray request form. Rather than being distinct photographs, radiographs are more like complex shadow-pictures which require expert interpretation. Knowing what the patient is complaining of or what his underlying medical problems are makes it easier to determine what the x-ray studies show.

"Yeah, big-time. Do you think it's pancreatitis?" Elise replied.

"Sure could be. No obstruction or free air. I don't see any kidney or gall stones, either," the thorough radiology resident finished up his interpretation.

"Thanks, Sanjiv. Can I take the films?" Elise asked.

"Let me dictate them and I'll bring them right out to you," Sanjiv countered.

"Great. See ya."


Elise returned to the E.D. and picked up Carter's chart. The laboratory results were affixed to the front and Elise looked at the read-outs. Her eyebrows raised and then a puzzled look settled on her attractive face.

"Katriona," Elise called out. She waited for her staff physician to respond and walked to Room Six. "Could I see you out here for a moment?"

Dr. Hewston walked out wiping her hands with a paper towel, which she discarded in a trash can under one of the charting desks.

"I was done anyway. Let me jot down some orders and I'll be with you straightaway," the attending said in her charming Irish brogue. She checked off several boxes and wrote the orders for I.V. fluids and some medication. She dropped the chart in the orders' box and turned to Elise. Katriona tucked a wisp of carrot-colored hair back into place and gave Elise her full attention.

"Carter's labs are weird," Elise declared.

"Let me see," Katriona said and accepted the chart from Elise. She thumbed through the lab sheets and thought out loud. "Okay, amylase and lipase are somewhat elevated. No surprise there. Alcohol level, fifty-two, also not unexpected. What do you find odd, Elise?"

"Well, that's part of it. Carter seems like he is more intoxicated than a fifty-two. And look at his bicarb on the BMP," Elise directed her.

"Hmmm, now that's curious. Why is he so acidotic? Did you get a gas?" Katriona asked.

"Not yet. Carter said someone gave him bad stuff. Do you think.." Elise began and was curtly interrupted by her alarmed staff.

"You'd better get an alcohol panel and serum osmolality. What did his fundi look like?" Katriona asked imperatively.

Sheepishly, Elise confessed she had failed to examine them.

"Let's go see him together," Katriona said as she led the way to Room Nine.

Their examination confirmed their fears. Carter's eye examination showed some swelling of the retina and abnormality of the optic disk.

"He was singing the Battle Hymn of the Republic - I thought he was just having flight of ideas. I didn't realize he was trying to tell me his eyes were bothering him," Elise berated herself as the two walked out of the room discussing the case.

"Okay, what is your assessment now, doctor?" Katriona prodded Elise gently.

"Somehow or another, Carter drank methanol with his booze. He said someone gave him some bad stuff. Maybe he was given some antifreeze. He has the classics signs and symptoms. He had signs of intoxication, abdominal pain, vomiting, eye findings and a high anion-gap metabolic acidosis. Up to eighty percent of methanol poisonings have pancreatitis," Elise detailed.

"And what would you like to do for him?" quizzed the attending.

"Man, if only Carter knew! He'd be taking methanol all the time! The drug of choice for methanol is ethanol," Elise chuckled.

"Correct. Contact pharmacy and have them get together a drip of intravenous alcohol to get Carter's level to somewhere between one hundred and one hundred and fifty milligrams per deciliter," Katriona directed.

"And I'll call the renal people and have them arrange for dialysis," Elise added.

"Splendid," the attending said. "Perhaps we should present this in interesting case conference."

"I'm just glad we weren't led astray by the amylase and lipase and thought Carter was just pancreatitis. Then we'd be doing this as an M+M ," Elise said referring to morbidity and mortality conference where doctors tried to learn from others' mistakes.

No one liked having cases go bad. No one liked missing key diagnoses. And, certainly, no one liked losing a patient.

Katriona trilled, "The only good M+M is a peanut M+M!"

"Amen!" Elise responded, and she took off to make arrangements. Lucky Carter would be around for many more interns to come.

# CHAPTER 7

Monday morning there was a notice in Elise's mailbox that the charts she had requested were ready. She zipped over to Medical Records and signed the charts out. She stuck the records in her briefcase and ran to the cafeteria to grab a bite before her one p.m. to eleven p.m. shift began.

Elise served up a heaping plate of salad and helped herself to a roll and a diet Pepsi. She grabbed a hospital newsletter and had just started reading a notice that one of the younger radiologists had passed away over the weekend, when Janice straddled the chair across from her.

"Hey, how's chiefdom going?"

Elise replied, "I nearly got called in on Saturday. The intern had misread the schedule and didn't show up for his shift. I was thrilled, considering I had worked till five am. Fortunately, he was home and was reachable. They managed for an hour without him."

"Interns can be more of a bother than a help, anyway," Janice commiserated. "I'm on a family practice rotation and sometimes I think it would be easier to do the workups myself. The story always is completely different when I talk to the patients."

"Tell me that is not the most annoying thing! And then the staff comes in and triple checks and they get a third version! Of course, the only thing worse is using an interpreter. How does, *'Blah blah blah blahdy blah-blah, blah blahdy-blahdy-blah blah blah'* in Slovenian translate into just 'No' in English?"

Janice pointed to the obituary in the newsletter. "Isn't that tragic about Doctor Morris?"

"I don't think I know who she was."

"She was a neuroradiologist," Janice stated.

"Oh, yeah, now I can place her. I knew she looked familiar," the emergency resident replied.

"She was the wife of my F.P. advisor, Doctor Romano. The gossip is she killed herself with an overdose. He's pretty broken up about it. What do you figure someone could be so depressed about when her husband just won thirty-eight million dollars in the lottery?" Janice informed her friend.

"No way?! He actually won the lottery? Is he still practicing? I'd be in Tahiti sipping fruity drinks with teeny tiny umbrellas in them all day long, having some cute, tan pool boy rub sunscreen on my back. Gee, is he in the market for a new wife?"

"Gross, Elise. I know you people in the E.D. have morbid senses of humor, but that's over the edge," Janice admonished her.

Elise gulped her last bite of her lunch and picked her soda off the tray. "Sorry. Well, I've got to go. Say hi to Don for me. I'll talk to you this week."

"Ciao, baby."


By one p.m., the attending and morning resident were eagerly awaiting the arrival of the swing shift resident. As usual, there were several patients waiting to be seen and Elise scanned the board.

The nurses maintained the large dry erase board that listed the room numbers, patients' last names, ages, genders, and chief complaints. It was usually pretty reliable to triage severity of illness from the chief complaints, although occasionally it could be deceptive. The accreditation body of hospitals proscribed writing the patient's problem in plain sight for confidentiality purposes, but they never had to keep track of fourteen sick and traumatized patients at the same time. So the medical staff disregarded the prohibition until review time, and they used a shorthand code system that, hopefully, only the medical personnel could interpret.

'CA $\bar{c}$ T' won for the most serious complaint waiting for evaluation. Medicine, in general, is fraught with abbreviations - it serves to confound patients and impede and aggravate lawyers. This particular one translated to '*Cancer patient with a fever*' which is often a true medical emergency.

Elise entered Room Three and was touched by the sight awaiting her. An emaciated thirty-four year old woman wearing a brightly colored scarf to conceal her baldness was being cradled by her distraught husband. The triage note stated that Mrs. Randolph had breast cancer and was receiving multiple chemotherapeutic agents following a modified radical mastectomy. Her temperature at the triage desk was 39.7° C. orally. Elise had to take out her calculator and figure out the Fahrenheit equivalent of 103.6°.

"When did the fever start?" she asked the patient.

"Last night she wasn't feeling well and didn't eat much. Around eight o'clock this morning she started having chills. I didn't know she had a fever until we got here," Mr. Randolph responded as he stroked his wife's cheek.

"Have you noticed any other symptoms, like a sore throat, cough, shortness of breath, chest pain, abdominal pain, burning on urination, or blood in the urine?" Elise again directed her questioning to Mrs. Randolph.

"She has a sore throat from the yeast, but that's not new and she uses lozenges for that. She has had a little dry cough," her husband answered protectively again.

"It hurts here when I breathe," Mrs. Randolph weakly added, motioning to her right upper chest.

"Has your access site been sore or red?" Elise was referring to a device the surgeons had implanted under Mrs. Randolph's skin to allow blood drawing and medication infusion without repeated venous punctures. These could get infected, and, in cancer patients who were immunocompromised, there might be very little visible evidence to this effect.

"No," she replied.

"We're going to have to do some blood tests, we'll need a urine sample and a chest x-ray. You are going to need antibiotics and we will have to keep you in the hospital."

Mrs. Randolph started sobbing quietly.

"I'm sorry, doctor. We do understand, it is just that we have two small children at home and my wife hates to waste a single minute away from them," Mr. Randolph explained.

Elise noted that Mrs. Randolph was not allergic to any medications, consulted her antibiotic guide and selected two powerful drugs to combat infection. She then handed the orders to

Nancy who had been standing at the head of the bed charting. As she walked out, Mr. Randolph followed her.

"Doctor, I just wanted to be sure that you knew my wife is DNR. Her breast cancer is metastatic and we are trying the chemo and radiation and we are even considering a bone marrow transplant. But we also don't want her to suffer needlessly. Please do everything you can for her, short of putting her on a ventilator."

"We will respect your decision, " Elise acknowledged. This case was extremely difficult for her as she remembered her mother lying on her deathbed, wasting away from premenopausal breast cancer. It also reminded her that she was long overdue to perform her own self-breast examination. *Doctors are the worst patients*, she thought and sighed.

She selected the next chart and opened the door to Room Ten.

"I'm Doctor Silver. What seems to be the problem today?"

An anxious looking African-American woman holding an eighteen month old child on her lap answered, " I think Bobbie ate some money."

Elise surveyed the child. Roberta Davis was smiling and clinging to her mother. She was having no difficulty breathing and seemed to be handling her secretions without difficulty. There were no coughing or gagging sounds.

"What makes you think that?"

"She was crawling on the floor and then I heard her cough and I thought I saw a flash of metal in her mouth."

Elise was skeptical. She listened to the baby's heart and lungs, looked in her mouth, and palpated her abdomen. The child giggled.

"Are you ticklish? Well, I don't see any evidence that she ate anything, but we will get an x-ray just to check."

"Jill, could you order a babygram on Room Ten, please?" Elise requested as she reached the nurses' station.

"Doctor Silver, I think I have..."

"Rich, could you try Elise?" In the emergency department, people did not stand on formalities.

"..a triple-A. Elise," her medical student blurted out breathlessly.

Elise looked at him sharply. "Tell me the story. The abridged version," she amended. Medical students often had a tendency to have difficulty distinguishing between important points and insignificant ones. Elise was not interested in the patient's childhood illnesses or bowel habits if the patient truly had a tear of his abdominal aorta.

Fortunately, Rich was an able fourth year medical student from Northwestern and was hoping to match in an emergency medicine residency. He had done a month of EM earlier in the year and was spending his vacation doing another two weeks in the hopes of sucking up enough to get into the Chicago General residency program. It had an excellent reputation in emergency medicine circles, and wouldn't require relocation.

"This is an eighty year old gentleman with a history of hypertension who had the acute onset of bad back pain approximately two hours ago, and now his left lower quadrant hurts. His heart rate is one hundred and twelve and he is clammy. His abdomen looks distended."

"Where is he?"

Rich started leading her to Room Two.

"Could you feel a pulsatile mass?"

"Well, no, but he's not exactly a thin guy," he explained.

They burst through the curtains. Elise glanced at the monitor which showed a sinus tachycardia. Rich was entirely accurate in his description of the patient, and Elise was afraid his assessment was right on target.

She asked the patient several questions about his urination and bowel movements, his past history, and the quality of the pain.

Mr. Flores was fidgeting on the bed, unable to find a comfortable position. He was involuntarily moaning and winced as she palpated his abdomen. It was swollen and the skin was mottled and cool. Elise was unable to appreciate a pulsating mass either, but she suspected it was due to the distention.

She took the chart out of the medical student's hands and jotted down orders, including two large sized intravenous lines with blood tubing and a request for eight units of blood. She quietly told Rich to have the vascular surgery resident paged STAT and to get him down here *now*.

"Mister Flores, I am very concerned that there is a problem with the largest artery in your body called the aorta. Sometimes..."

Mr. Flores cut her off, "Oh, yeah, I have an aneurysm."

She was surprised. *Remarkable the things that slip your mind when you are asked, in the course of taking a medical history*, "Do you have any medical problems?"

"How big is it?"

"Five centimeters," he answered knowledgeably.

"Well, I am very concerned that it has torn and is leaking blood. We are going to have to get you to surgery right away. You don't happen to know your blood type, do you?"

"A positive. Can I see my daughter?"

"Certainly, is she here or do we need to call her?"

"She's in the waiting room," answered Monica who had come into the room to carry out the doctors' orders.

"I'll get her myself," offered Elise.

She went out and outlined the situation to Mr. Flores' daughter. She was understandably upset, but promised to put on a brave front for her father's sake.

Fifteen minutes after the fourth year surgical resident doing his vascular surgery rotation arrived, Mr. Flores was wheeled off to the O.R. with two units of O positive blood pouring into his veins. Elise said a silent prayer that they would be in time.


*I'll be damned*, she thought as she examined Bobbie's x-ray. There, sitting in the stomach, was a metallic foreign body the size and shape of a nickel. Bobbie's mother was relieved when Elise explained that it would pass through her intestinal system without difficulty, but was dismayed when she realized how she had to check for it.

"Yuck! We ain't that poor! Girl, don't be putting things in your mouth again!" she reprimanded her child as they left with their instructions.

Mrs. Randolph's radiographs were back and Elise called the junior resident and medical student over to examine the beautifully demonstrated pneumonia underlying the precise area where the patient had stated she had pain. Her first doses of antibiotics had already been infused. Elise had chosen ones which would treat all different types of infections, including pneumonias. Mrs. Randolph felt somewhat better after her fever had responded to acetaminophen and she was admitted to the oncology floor for further treatment.

When the department had slowed sufficiently that Elise had time to eat her dinner, she also took the opportunity to xerox the two charts of the identically shaped brain hemorrhages so she could review them at her leisure at home. She figured confidentiality problems probably didn't apply to deceased patients, and put the original charts in the charts' basket to be returned to the medical records department in the morning.

Suddenly, a commotion broke out in the waiting room. Elise and her staff, Dr. Vakesh Patel, poked their heads out to see what was going on. There were about twenty patients standing on line by triage, complaining about having to wait. The ambulance doors opened up and Elise joined the paramedics in Room Five while Vakesh sorted out the trouble in front.

It turned out to be related. John McKnight and Stan Stykler wheeled their patient in and transferred her to the gurney.

"Hi, Johnny. Hey, Stickler. What's shaking?" Elise asked.

"The usual. Bus accident," answered the burly black medic.

"How many were hurt? Are we going to need to call a disaster?" Elise asked anxiously. A disaster plan was called when a large accident occurred and the number of patients resulting was likely to overwhelm the system. Patients would be distributed to multiple hospitals to avoid overloading a single facility. The plan detailed the mechanism to recruit additional help from the rest of the hospital and from personnel at home, if need be. Elise had only been through one real disaster, an El train derailment, but had been involved in many disaster drills over the course of her residency.

"Doubt it. Only this lady was hurt. She was standing in the front, putting her money in the machine, when the bus was smashed on the driver's side. She went flying out the door. Unfortunately, the door happened to be closed at the time," Stickler continued.

*Well, that explains all the lacerations and the cervical collar and backboard.* Elise started to cut the patient's clothes off but was relieved by Chris.

"How many people were on the bus?" Elise asked.

Stickler and Johnny laughed.

"Like, what difference does that make?" Johnny asked.

Elise and Chris looked at him askance.

The boys in blue explained.

"When there is a CTA accident, people push their way on the bus through the rear door..." Stickler began before Elise interrupted him.

"Wait, a minute, you mean off the bus, don't you?" she corrected.

"No, I mean *on* the bus. Don't you see? It's lottery time. There is no record of who was actually on the bus at the time of the accident, so the transit authority gives everyone a small settlement without a lot of legal hassle. Everyone and his brother jumps on the bus and claims whiplash," Stickler finished.

"How do you know who's really hurt and needs to be transported here?" Elise asked curiously.

Johnny grunted and answered, "That's easy. We get on the bus and say, 'Whoever needs to go to the hospital, get off the bus and stand over there.' Whoever is too injured to answer or get off, we take 'em."

Elise shook her head and evaluated her new patient. Miraculously, she turned out to have no serious internal injuries and her spine was not broken. She did, however, take almost the rest of the shift for Elise to pick out the accessible glass shards and suture up her cuts. The diligent resident explained to the injured passenger that the rest of the glass pieces would either stay put and cause no trouble, remain inside and develop infection necessitating further procedures to remove them, or they would just work their way out naturally. Elise further counseled her that it takes up to six months to tell the final extent of a scar and that plastic surgery could perform revisions if needed.

Just before her shift ended, Scott Rick came by to report that the surgery on Mr. Flores was over, and he had at least made it to the intensive care unit.

"Doctor Rosenberg let me sew most of the graft," he boasted. "And Mister Flores moved his legs as he came out from the anesthesia!"

Dr. Rick went on to explain to the junior members of the medical team that, in the course of repairing an abdominal aortic aneurysm, the surgeons had to clamp off the large vessel to stop the loss of blood. In the process, there is an artery that supplies the spinal cord which may be affected. If there is too little flow through it, for too long a period of time, the patient may survive the operation only to find he is paralyzed from the waist down.

Elise complimented Scott on his success and lauded Rich for his quick and accurate assessment. "Rich, you saved someone's life tonight. There is no greater reward in emergency medicine. Excellent job!"

Rich beamed. It was so rare that anyone gave you positive reinforcement in this profession. Everyone was eager to tell you what you had done wrong or if a patient complained about your care, but being thanked or praised was hard to come by. And it was especially nice to end your shift on that note!

# CHAPTER 8

*I just don't understand it*, Elise thought. *This physical examination is simply not consistent with the outcome of death.*

As she lounged about in her sweats, drinking coffee in her dining area, she reread Mr. Weber's physical examination as Neil Anderson had documented it.

> *79 yo WM (= year old white male*; Elise mentally translated the abbreviations as she went along*) well developed, well nourished, in no acute distress.*
> <u>*Skin*</u>*: No signs of trauma.*
> <u>*Head, ears, eyes, nose and throat*</u>*: Right sided facial droop, cataracts noted but pupils equal in size. Tongue deviates to right.*
> <u>*Neck*</u>*: No bruits. Resists movement laterally.*
> <u>*Lungs*</u>*: Clear.*
> <u>*Heart:*</u> *Regular with mechanical click.*
> <u>*Abdomen*</u>*: Normal.*
> <u>*Extremities*</u>*: No cyanosis, clubbing or edema. Tone and strength normal.*
> <u>*Neurological:*</u> *Alert and oriented. Cranial nerves as above. Dysarthria noted. Reflexes normal. No Babinski.*

Elise read her own droppings, her affectionate term for notations that a senior resident or attending physician added to a junior's chart for completeness' sake.

> *Unable to visualize fundi secondary to cataracts. No meningeal signs. No pronator drift.*

Dr. Weinfeld's note did not add anything substantive either. He had not seen the patient prior to the cardiac arrest, and his documentation was mostly regarding the resuscitation attempts.

There was very little in the exam to suggest a stroke of such magnitude that someone would die from it. She looked at the time course. Four hours after presentation to the E.D., Mr. Weber died. *Maybe he had a small bleed that extended just before C.T. scan.* She checked the nurse's notes.

*Now that's really odd*, she thought.

> *1445 hrs: Patient returned from C.T. scan. Pupils equal and react to light. Patient requesting lunch. Instructed he would have to wait until MD approval.*
>
> *1530 hrs: BP 165/92, HR 88, RR 18 and nonlabored.*

A monitor strip showing a normal heart rhythm was taped to the nurses' notes after this entry. The record continued.

> *1540 hrs: Up to bathroom with assist. Gait wide based but steady.*
>
> *1550 hrs: PMD (*private medical doctor*) with patient.*
>
> *1608 hrs: Went to check on patient and found him in cardiac arrest. See Code sheet.*

And that concluded the regular nurses' notes. The documentation of the resuscitative efforts was on a separate sheet designed for that purpose. Elise read it over as well. It seemed pretty unremarkable. Mr. Weber had been given standard ACLS treatment.

*How could the C.T. scan have shown such a tremendous hemorrhage and Mr. Weber be asking for lunch?! He should have been in a coma with those C.T. findings. There is something seriously wrong with this picture.*

She reviewed the other patient, Mr. Babcock's, course. He had been found unconscious at home by his wife, presented to the emergency department by ambulance, and only survived a half hour after being scanned. *Now his examination was consistent with his brain scan!*

Reviewing Mr. Weber's chart jogged Elise's memory and she remembered that Sid Shulman had personally come down to see Mr. Weber in the E.D. She also specifically recalled Mr. Weber's doting grandson. He had great blue eyes, a nice smile, and seemed sincerely upset when she broke the news of his grandfather's death. She remembered that he had told her he was a chemist and had supposedly gone to his lab.

*Hmmm, I wonder what kind of chemist he is? What kind of chemicals does he have access to? And what kind of inheritance did Grandpa leave him? That's so lame, you've been reading too many Kellerman novels!*

She pondered this for a while and then boldly picked up the telephone receiver. She found the next of kin line and noted Eric Weber's number was the same as the deceased's telephone number. After the answering machine tone, she identified herself and left her telephone number, asking Eric to return her call at his convenience.


Putting her day off to good use, Elise did her laundry and food shopping. She prided herself in being able to accomplish more in one day than most males could do in a week. As she brought her groceries in and set them on the kitchen counter, she noted her machine was blinking.

She rewound the tape and listened as she unpacked. Janice called to see what she was doing for dinner, Jodi, the E.D. clerk, was calling to remind her about a baby shower for one of the nurses, and the last message was from Eric Weber.

"This is Eric Weber. I am returning your call and see that you like playing telephone tag. Well, you're it!"

She smiled. *I really hope I'm wrong about him.*

She rummaged around for the chart and dialed his number again. The phone rang twice and then she heard his voice.

"Hello?"

"Mister Weber, this is Doctor Elise Silver. I'm sure you don't remember me but I was one of the physicians who took care of your grandfather when he was at Chicago General in August."

"I remember you very well, doctor. What can I do for you?"

"Well, this is rather awkward, but I was wondering if you would be available to talk to me, " Elise said as she was thankful that video phones were not in vogue yet. Her bright red cheeks might have revealed more than she cared to.

"I would be happy to. If I could be so bold, have you eaten yet?"

"No," she answered.

"Oh, you probably have plans..."

"No, I don't!" *Damn, I sounded way too eager*, Elise regretted her quick response.

"Great. Would you like to talk over dinner?" Eric asked.

"That would be fine," she replied in a more restrained tone.

"How does six-thirty sound?"

"Sounds perfect."

"Would you like me to pick you up or would you prefer to meet at the restaurant? And what do you like eating?"

Elise wondered if it was a mistake to let him pick her up, probably so if he turned out to be a cold-blooded murderer. She decided to take a chance and gave him her address. It happened that they had similar dining preferences and they agreed upon Italian.

Elise showered and tossed three rejected outfits on her bed before she finally settled on a colorful sweater and black leggings. She pulled on her favorite black boots and finished up with earrings and a light application of makeup to bring out her eyes.

At six-thirty, the doorbell rang. *I love a man who is prompt*, she thought approvingly.

"I'll be right down," Elise said into the intercom and then she grabbed her leather coat. The elevator was thankfully quick and Elise met him in the lobby. The grandson was wearing a burgundy turtleneck and black jeans which demonstrated his fit physique. The only jewelry he wore was a gold watch with an intricate face showing the date, military time around the periphery, and the phases of the moon. His smile gave Elise the same feeling she got from eating a pralines and cream hot fudge sundae while watching reruns of Babylon 5 in front of a crackling fire.

"Thanks for agreeing to meet with me, Mister Weber," Elise began.

Eric cut her off. "Could we forego the formalities and make it Eric, please?"

"Only if you call me Elise."

*She has a killer smile*, Eric thought. *I can't believe she called me.*

They made small talk on the way to the restaurant in his Camry. As the valet drove off, Eric and Elise mounted the stairs and entered Luigi's.

Elise had never been to this restaurant before and Eric explained it looked like a dive, but the food was divine. The maitre'd greeted them and it was obvious that Eric was well known there. They were shown to a private corner table in the no smoking section, and the maitre'd held out Elise's seat for her.

They perused the menu and Eric made some recommendations. The waiter described the specials and lit a candle in the center of the cliché red and white checkered tablecloth. Elise was mildly impressed at Eric's Italian accent as he ordered for both of them. The waiter brought a bottle of Chianti over and Eric tasted it and nodded. The waiter poured two ample glasses and retreated to get the breadbasket and garlic flavored olive oil.

"I must make a confession. I don't care what you want to talk about, I'm just really glad you called me. The circumstances of our meeting were pretty awful, but I have to admit I was attracted to you. I would never have had the nerve to contact you," Eric shared as he looked down, afraid to meet Elise's eyes.

"I'm flattered. How have you been doing since your grandfather passed away?" Elise felt her heart pounding as she discovered the attraction was mutual.

"I'm okay. I was very close to my grandfather. I lived with him ever since my parents died when I was fourteen."

Eric continued to describe the accident which had orphaned him. He told Elise that he was an only child and his grandparents had done everything to make him feel loved and safe. His grandmother had died of colon cancer two years before and he had supported his grandfather in his time of need. Eric had been out of town for several days prior to his grandfather's demise, and had returned late that morning to find a note stating he had been taken to C.G.H.

Elise tactfully explored the financial situation, trying to establish a possible motive. Jefferey Weber had worked all his life and made quite a success of a dry cleaning business. He had four stores and had started pick-up and delivery service at downtown offices many years before. Eric confided that his grandfather was too trusting and had used a financial planner who had given him some very bad advice and taken advantage of him. Mr. Weber lost quite a deal of money and was left comfortable, but that was all. Eric was left their home and a modest sum of money and C.G.H. was to receive the rest.

"PopPop gave C.G.H. many years of service, first as a volunteer, and eventually on the board. He wanted to support it in the only way he knew how. It saddened him to know that all the money he expected to have for his golden years, and beyond, had been lost. He was pretty embarrassed about being taken in by that shyster financial planner so he really didn't let anyone know he was in that predicament. I think the other members of the board will be a bit surprised to see how little PopPop really had to leave when the estate is finally settled."

Elise segued into Eric's work.

"I got a master's in chemistry and landed a job with Clark-Davies in their quality improvement department. I manage the section now. Basically, we ensure that the drugs we produce are pure."

"What kind of drugs do you make?" she inquired.

"Lots of different one. Antibiotics, cardiac drugs, you name it, we have a product on the market," Eric named several pharmaceuticals Elise recognized and used in her practice. "But enough about me. Why did you go into emergency medicine?"

"I love what I do. Every patient has something different and you never know what is going to come in the door next. Emergency medicine's like a big puzzle. If you ask the right questions, listen to the answers, and pay attention to abnormalities on the physical and in the lab results, you figure out what is wrong with most of the patients."

They ate possibly the best Italian meal Elise had ever had as they talked. Eric raved at how good the food tasted after just getting over the flu and being unable to keep anything down for twenty-four hours. Elise marveled at the ease with which they conversed; there were no uneasy silences as one might have on a first date.

She reprimanded herself immediately for allowing that thought to cross her mind, *this isn't really a date!*

Eric continued to ask many questions about Elise's life and work, and seemed to be extremely attentive. His listening skills were flawless and Elise found herself sharing thoughts and memories long submerged.

As they sipped cappuccino and shared a tiramisu, Eric asked, "Elise, what exactly prompted you to call me? I'd love to think that you couldn't get me out of your mind since the moment we met, but I'm not that conceited. And I am more than a little curious."

Elise took a deep breath. Her thoughts had shifted from intrigue to romance. *Well, if this doesn't blow it, I guess nothing will.*

"Eric, I was going through x-rays for a conference and I discovered something very odd. Your grandfather's C.T. scan is identical to another patient's scan which was done several years ago. I mean exactly the same, which is basically impossible. So I reviewed his chart and there are inconsistencies which lead me to believe there may have been foul play. I was hoping you might be able to shed some light on his situation and help me figure this out."

There seemed no good reason to let Eric know he was basically her only suspect.

Elise watched Eric for his response. There was nothing to suggest a guilty conscience; on the contrary, Eric looked alarmed.

"What do you think?"

"I'm wondering who could have and would have murdered your grandfather. Do you have any ideas? Did he have any enemies?"

Eric shook his head. "Not that I can think of. Is it possible that there was a mix-up in the x-ray department and you never saw the right films?"

"I guess that is a possibility. I hadn't thought of it. But then I have no explanation as to why he died."

Eric swiftly slid his credit card into the check holder. He waved off her offer to split the bill.

"I think the best thing to do now is give me some time to think and we should get together, say this weekend, to see if I can think of any suspects for you," he said seriously, with a glint in his eye.

Elise's heart did flip-flops and she smiled.

"Well, I'm off Saturday and don't have to be at work until Sunday at one p.m. Do you think that will give you enough time?"

"Uh, you're sure there isn't anyone else who will object to my occupying your Saturday night?"

Elise laughed. "What a tactful way to ask. No, I am currently unattached and my cat spends lots of time alone. He can handle it. How about you?'

"No. I don't have a cat." He paused for comic effect. "No, it's been a while since I was in any kind of serious relationship," he replied.


They ransomed his car from the valet, and Eric walked Elise up to her stairs when they arrived at her apartment building.

"I really enjoyed tonight. Maybe it wasn't murder, but fate that had us meet, " Eric said. "Man, that was pretty corny, huh?"

"Thank you for dinner. It was wonderful. And I really enjoyed being with you, too," Elise stammered.

*Ah, the first awkward moment. It almost felt like they should kiss, but no way! It was way too soon, and besides, who wanted a twenty-four hour stomach flu bug?!* Elise unlocked the front door and waved as Eric walked to his car.

As the mildly infatuated resident peeled off her garments, she pondered her evening. *He's handsome and secure, lonely and I rather think he's attracted to me, too. But don't you think you need to get to know him better? He certainly doesn't seem like someone who could kill, or even orchestrate the murder of, his own grandfather, for any reason. Oh yeah, and just how many murderers do you know intimately?!*

Elise's inner voices argued until the waning moon set and sleep deprivation overwhelmed her obsessive-compulsive nature to reason everything out to the bitter end. Ultimately, the only conclusion she could come to was she was eager to see him again.

# CHAPTER 9

"Call x-ray and see what's taking so long for that portable, please," Elise called across the department.

Elise reviewed the facts with her attending, Dr. Lillian, and the medical student, Jason Hawkins.

"Fifty year old black male with a history of prostate cancer and no other medical history, had acute onset of shortness of breath approximately one hour ago. There was no obvious precipitating factor. He did have a sharp pain on the right side of his chest but it doesn't sound cardiac in nature. It increases on respirations, but isn't really affected by movement. His heart rate is one hundred and twenty-six and his respirations are thirty-two, but his lungs are clear. There is no edema of the extremities."

Dr. Lillian nodded and turned to Jason, "What is the differential diagnosis?"

"Well, it could be something to do with his heart, like a heart attack or failure, but he has no history of it and the chest pain would be atypical. It could be emphysema or asthma, but again, no history. Maybe a pneumothorax?" he hypothesized.

Elise countered, "But he has normal breath sounds so a collapsed lung is less likely. What lab tests might be helpful?"

"A chest x-ray and a blood gas for sure. Maybe a C.B.C., oh, and an E.K.G.," he offered.

The whirring of the portable x-ray machine grew louder as it approached the doctors. Elise signaled to the med student to follow as she continued, "The blood gas showed low oxygen even in the face of supplemental oxygen. We will soon see what the x-ray shows."

Elise turned to the radiology technologist and asked, "Charlie, how's it going?"

"Good, Doc, how are you?" The tall, bearded man always had a smile on his face and seemed eager to do a good job. He rarely needed to take a second shot.

"Fine, thanks. Hey, can I ask you a question?"

"You can ask two!" he said, as he placed the cold film cassette behind Mr. White's back.

"When you are working in C.T. scan, how does the patient's name get on the films?" Elise asked.

"We type it in at the beginning on the patient information parameters screen," he answered as he motioned to the physicians to take their reproductive organs out of the room so he could shoot his film safely. "Take a deep breath and hold it," he commanded the patient. A high-pitched squeak signaled the taking of the x-ray. "Breathe," Charlie commanded as he lurched forward to remove the film cassette.

"Is there a way of telling which radiology tech took the films?" she asked as she reentered the room.

They walked together towards the exit.

"Every film has some mark which identifies who performed the study, even portables. At our hospital, we put our number down under the date on C.T. studies. There is a master list of numbers to identify who has which number."

Elise wondered out loud, "What if someone forgot to do that?"

"Well, that would be quite unusual, but you could check who was scheduled in C.T. that day, I suppose. One of the things they ingrain in you at school is to follow proper procedure in marking the studies."

Charlie parked the machine next to the E.D. and strode off to develop the x-ray. As Elise walked back through the sliding doors into the department, she decided she would find the tech and question him or her regarding Mr. Weber's C.T. scan and unravel the mystery of the identical films.

She made several notations on a chart, and then Charlie returned with the x-ray and placed it on the reading board.

"Hmmm, just as I expected, " Elise murmured.

"I don't get it, " Jason said. "What's wrong with it? It looks pretty normal to me."

"Exactly!" Elise agreed. "What could make him look so uncomfortable with a normal looking film?"

Jason's forehead furrowed as he thought. "A P.E.?" he asked tentatively.

"Very good. He has prostate cancer which could make him a set-up for a pulmonary embolism. We'd better give him heparin to prevent further clotting in his lung and get a ventilation-perfusion scan to confirm our diagnosis. Could you please do a rectal to make sure there's no blood in his stool? Then, let's discuss our suspicion and anticoagulation with him and his family, and admit him to the unit," Elise answered.

Elise walked to the viewing board and shuffled through the folders until she found Mr. Creskin's films. She placed them on the light box and noted the boxer's fracture.

"Jason, are you done?" Elise asked as she caught a glimpse of the intern around the corner.

"I have to hand in the chart with the admission orders, but otherwise I'm done. Why? What do you have?" Jason responded.

"Come into Room Twelve when you are done," Elise suggested.

The pretty resident clipped the x-rays on the view box in the Cast Room. Mr. Creskin was sitting on the chair in the corner, with his right arm elevated on a pillow. Elise asked him to sit on the cart and moved the bedside table to support the pillow.

Jason entered the room and Elise introduced him as a rotating medical student.

"When you look at Mister Creskin's hand, what do you notice?" Elise quizzed.

Jason replied, "There is swelling and bruising over the hand at the base of the little finger and a small wound."

"Good," Elise encouraged. "What questions do you want to ask the patient?"

"I'd like to know which hand he writes with," Jason offered.

"Good. Mister Creskin is right-hand dominant. Anything else you would like to know?" Elise prompted.

"What he does for a living?" the student asked.

"Okay, he is a construction worker, so being able to use his hands is important to him. What else?" continued the pimping.

Jason thought for a moment.

"I guess I want to know how it happened."

"Me, too. Mister Creskin, you told the triage nurse you punched a wall. I need you to understand something. I will not be judgmental, but it is very important that I know the truth. If your fist came in contact with someone's teeth, a very serious infection could have been introduced into your hand. So I'm going to ask you again, is there any chance you punched someone in the mouth that caused this injury?"

Mr. Creskin averted his eyes and looked at his radiographs for a moment. Sheepishly, he looked down at the floor and answered, "Well, it is possible that I did this last night at a bar in a fight, and not on the wall earlier today."

"Jason, note the tiny radioopaque foreign body here? That could be a chip off the bone, or it could be a tiny piece of tooth teeming with organisms," the resident instructed. She turned her attention back to the patient, "Okay, I'm going to call the hand experts and they will be down to finish taking care of you, Mister Creskin. Thanks for being honest with me," Elise said.

She continued talking to Jason on the way out, "It is especially bad if the joint space has been violated. He'll need to be on I.V. antibiotics. I have a feeling they will need to explore him and clean him out."


"Somebody help him!" came a muffled scream from the waiting room.

Elise shouted, "Grab a gurney!" to a passing nurse and burst out the glass sliding doors, with Jason in tow.

She found a young black teenager, probably fourteen or so, in a crumpled heap on the wheelchair ramp. She noted a pool of dark red blood beneath him. As she, Jason, Jackie, and two security guards carefully lifted the slender teen onto the cart, she asked if anyone had witnessed what had happened. She ascertained that two other teens, one light skinned African-American and one Latino, wearing flashy sports jackets had callously dumped the unconscious injured boy out of a shiny, jet black Ford Expedition and sped off.

*Another example of senseless gang violence undoubtedly*, Elise speculated.

They rushed the cart into Room One, whose previous occupant had been shuttled into the hall until another vacant room was made available. Overhead, the hospital P.A. system boomed, "Trauma team to the Emergency Department, Trauma team to the Emergency Department!"

Silently Jackie and Janet cut the boy's clothes off with heavy-duty trauma scissors which had been purchased for each nurse last Emergency Nurses' Day. They took care to cut along the seams and would avoid any bullet holes or tears from a stabbing. The clothes would be brown paper bagged and tagged and would stay with the patient or a police officer to maintain the chain of evidence. The child was placed on a cardiac monitor and a rigid cervical collar was applied to prevent movement of his neck, as per protocol. His vital signs were taken as Elise surveyed the situation.

*ABCs*, Elise mentally reviewed. *A - Airway. His airway is open, I don't hear any stridor. B - Breathing, his rate is rapid and shallow.* She listened to his lungs and was pleased to hear breath sounds on both sides.

She resumed, *C for Circulation.* "What are his vital signs?"

Janet, a tall brunette nurse with fifteen years of emergency nursing experience replied without looking up, "Heart rate, one hundred fifty and regular, respiratory rate is forty and shallow, and BP... I need the Doppler."

The P.C.T., Steve, scrambled into the Gyne room to find the electronic device. Although its most common usage in Chicago General E.D. was to hear fetal heart tones, it was also used to measure very low blood pressure and check for weak pulses.

Elise continued her systematic analysis. *Are there any external signs of bleeding? What does his heart sound like?*

She scrutinized the nude form as the members of the trauma team arrived. Joel Jansen, M.D., the trauma fellow, joined her at the side of the gurney to assess the situation. She quickly ran through the particulars for him and they began issuing commands. Elise instructed her junior resident to place a large, long intravenous line into the large vein in the boy's groin while Jackie inserted an I.V. into a large vein in his arm. Dave Gomez, D.O., the EM resident, handed Jackie two large syringes with enough blood to send off a trauma panel. Charlie was requested to take a complete set of trauma films. Joel had Scott Rick, M.D. do the primary survey while the respiratory therapy student grabbed an ABG from an unoccupied limb.

"Scott, how does it feel?" Joel asked as the fourth-year resident palpated the prostate on rectal exam.

"Normal. Not high riding or boggy. The pelvic rock was negative," he replied professionally, suppressing the urge to give his senior a smart ass answer.

"Jason, stick a Foley in," Elise commanded, trying to let the student feel involved.

"Now we have intravenous access above and below the diaphragm," Elise noted. "Why might that be important?"

The resident who was drawing an arterial blood gas answered assuredly, "So in case there is an interruption of the venous return to the heart, we have a better chance of administering fluids successfully."

Jason face flushed and he said anxiously, "Uh-oh," after the Foley was passed. Very bloody urine was being collected in the bag. "Did I do something wrong?"

"No, you did fine," responded the trauma fellow kindly. "Looks like he bagged his kidney, Elise."

Elise nodded in assent. She asked Joel, "I think I should intubate him, do you agree?"

He did and she maneuvered into place at the head of the bed to insert the tube to assist his breathing. Steve held the boy's head stable to prevent movement of the neck in case of spine fracture. As Elise placed the tube, she remarked, "I have yet to find the site of injury. He doesn't look beaten, I'm guessing gun shot from the amount of blood we saw out on the sidewalk."

"Judging from the hematuria, added to the fact that his belly is distended and hard, I would guess one to the abdomen at very least," he concurred.

After the surgical resident completed his line, he finished his secondary survey to try to appraise the extent of the damage. He discovered that there was no movement of any extremity, even to painful stimuli, and reflexes were absent.

"We'd better roll him," Joel replied.

Carefully, the residents placed their arms under the patient and in a fluid motion, on the count of three, turned him as a single unit, on his side to view his back. Scott pointed out an amateurish upside-down trident tattoo on the right shoulder confirming Elise's suspicion of gang involvement. Janet announced loudly, "Look at the monitor!" as it began to alarm, heralding an erratic heartbeat.

"Crap!" Elise exclaimed, "On three…"

In unison, they returned the teen to his original supine position, but not before they had all visualized the two bullet wounds wreaking the havoc. There was one to the back of the neck and one to his right flank. There had been no further significant external blood loss which suggested internal bleeding as the cause of the boy's shocky condition.

"Defibrillate at two hundred joules," Elise ordered and the student positioned himself to comply. "How much fluid has he received?"

"Two liters of lactated ringers," replied Janet. "His blood pressure was sixty by Doppler before he went into V. fib."

"Get two units of O positive blood and have them get ten units of type specific or crossmatched blood ready. We'd better crack his chest. If we can't shock him out of fib, we'll be able to do internal defibrillation, " decided Joel.

"How many have you done?" Elise quickly surveyed the residents.

The emergency medicine resident had only done one whereas the more senior surgical resident who had already rotated on thoracic surgery had done more. Elise directed Scott to supervise Dave in the thoracotomy and listened as he detailed the procedure.

They gloved up and rapidly prepared their instruments to violate the boy's chest cavity.

"Clear!" said Jason loudly as he glanced around, making sure no one was touching the patient or the bed. He ensured that the paddles were applied against the gel pads with the requisite pressure and discharged the machine. The adolescent's body jerked up off the bed reflexively.

Without waiting to see the results, Dave whipped off the pads and slopped some Betadine on the left lateral chest. He made a deft incision from breastbone to left side avoiding the nipple. Another slice with the scalpel and the doctors inserted the retracting device to spread the ribs apart. The medical student watched with respectful awe. Elise's hands itched to perform it herself. It was considerably harder to supervise a less experienced resident, than to just do the job yourself. Everyone had to learn sometime, but there would be little tolerance for error or sloth in the case of a fourteen-year-old boy. Elise and Joel would have no qualms about intervening if necessary.

"Why do you suppose we are doing this if we don't believe the pathology is in the chest?" Elise quizzed Jason.

He hesitated and Scott answered for him, "Because we suspect he is losing massive amounts of blood in his belly. This way we will block arterial blood flow to the lower part of the body and try to preserve perfusion to the most vital organs, the heart, lungs, and brain."

The initial defibrillation had restored the heartbeat to a normal, albeit rapid, one. The physicians were now in position, however, to do open heart massage if the need arose.

"The O.R. is ready whenever you are and Doctor Hassan is scrubbing as we speak," Dr. Lillian said as he stepped past the curtain.

"Boy, are we lucky it's Hassan!" said Joel quietly to Elise. "He is the most technically skilled trauma surgeon we have here, and he has a pleasant disposition to boot. That's probably one of the only accurate things they show on *ER*- the asshole surgeon mentality."

Elise rolled her eyes and agreed. That T.V. show drove her crazy sometimes. Some situations were so unrealistic and then real-life patients came in to her E.D. with dumb expectations. *Like as if I could ever get anyone to V/Q scan in under four hours! Or do bone marrow biopsies and institute chemotherapy regimens by myself!*

"Yeah, that and the green stuff growing on the food in the fridge!" she added, laughing.

The young doctors inserted the instruments to clamp off the aorta to prevent wasted blood flow into the abdomen. His blood pressure rose to 90/40 but he was still critical. They unceremoniously tossed a sheet over the boy as the nurses hastily disconnected tubes and wires in preparation for transport to the operating suite.

Charlie showed the senior physicians the films. Two bullets were seen; one had shattered two vertebrae in the boy's neck, and one was noted in the upper right abdomen. The endotracheal and nasogastric tubes were in good position and the lungs were clear.

The surgical entourage wheeled the gurney out to the corridor leading to the surgical suite. Elise eyed the trauma room. *What a disaster area!* It looked like a scene straight out of one of those Halloween horror flicks. Paper wrappings, towels, tubes, gauze were strewn all about and there was a deep, clotting pool of blood radiating maroon tracks where the gurney's wheels had dragged the boy's life substance.

Elise looked at her watch. Twenty-two minutes had elapsed. She steeled herself for her next duty. She had been informed that the boy's mother had arrived. The woman only knew that her son had been shot, but was completely unaware of the severity of his injuries. Elise waited for the pastoral care representative and they walked out to the quiet room together. Of all her responsibilities, this was the one she loathed the most.

# CHAPTER 10

The next night she related the story to Eric.

"I hate to say it, but maybe he's lucky he didn't make it. His spinal cord was severed. The right kidney undoubtedly couldn't be salvaged and he probably would have lost the function in the other from prolonged aortic clamping. Quadriplegic and on permanent hemodialysis, not my idea of a full life."

Elise sipped her sweet dessert wine. She rubbed her eyes wearily. Eric waited patiently for her to continue.

"You know what the most distressing thing to me was?" she said rhetorically. "His mother wasn't outraged that her son, her thirteen year old baby, had been shot. I'd have been crazy out of my mind, but these people get inured to it. It's not that she didn't care, it's just that she didn't find it surprising or even unexpected. This is the second child she's lost to gang violence. He was only thirteen."

Eric placed his hand on Elise's and gently squeezed. She gratefully raised her glistening eyes and met his caring gaze.

She collected herself and gave him a half smile. "Enough of that. How would you like to help me do some sleuthing?"

"What did you have in mind?"

"I checked your grandfather's C.T. scan. There is a number which identifies which technologist performed the study and I want to see who it is. The nun who runs Radiology might give me a hard time if I try figuring it out during business hours. If we do it now, we may be able to bypass some of the bureaucratic red tape," Elise explained.

Eric paid the bill and helped Elise on with her coat. His hand lightly lingered on her shoulder and she subtly leaned towards him. They descended the stairs in comfortable silence and walked two blocks to get Eric's car.

"I really can't imagine anyone harming PopPop. He was such a kind, generous, loving human being. He gave your hospital a great deal of his time, and money. He always paid shiva calls to people from temple. Every Christmas he would roll up his sleeves and serve dinner at an inner city soup kitchen. He once made me go to the neighborhood 7-11 at ten o'clock at night when he emptied his pockets for bed and discovered that the clerk had mistakenly given him change for a twenty instead of a ten when he bought his lottery ticket that afternoon."

He held the door open for Elise as she got in the passenger side. He slid into his seat, fastened his seatbelt, and drove to Chicago General Hospital.

Elise greeted the uniformed security guard who waved the couple past. They walked through the older section of the hospital to get to the new part which housed Radiology, the revamped Emergency Department, and the ICUs. Elise led Eric down the darkened corridor and called out to locate the radiology tech.

"Hey, Chaz, glad you're here," Elise acknowledged as he approached. "You working p.m.s tonight?"

Charlie explained, "I'm working a double. Christmas cometh and all."

Elise introduced Eric and filled Charlie in on their mission.

"Remember I asked you about identifying a tech who did a scan?" she reminded him.

Elise slipped her duplicate film out of its folder. She pointed out the number and asked him whose it was.

Charlie led them to the computer and punched the keyboard until he had brought up the necessary list.

"Now let's see. Fifty-eight..., " he said as he perused the list. "There is no fifty-eight currently working. Let me call up the master list which has all past and present personnel on it."

Several minutes went by as Charlie searched through the files. He remarked, "Sorry it's taking me so long. This department really misses Linda. She was our computer whiz. Fifty-eight, that was assigned to Diane Coates. She hasn't worked here since spring of nineteen ninety-six when she moved to Arizona. Someone must have entered the wrong number accidentally. Let's see who was working that day."

The amiable technologist walked over to another desk and brought back over a loose-leaf notebook. He flipped through the pages which held the schedules of the past year. He stopped at the week in question and scanned down until he found August twenty-fourth.

"What time does it say? Okay, day shift," he murmured to himself. "Well, that's bizarre!"

"What?" Elise asked eagerly.

"*I* was the tech on C.T. that day. My number is one twenty-seven and I couldn't have typed in fifty-eight by mistake. I suppose I could have been on lunch at that time. Either Julia or Miles would have been covering. Let's see, Julia is...number seventy-nine and Miles is...one hundred and sixteen. Well, that doesn't make any sense. I have no idea how this happened," Charlie said with a frown on his usually cheerful fuzzy face.

Elise asked, "Who were the doctors working that day?"

"Linda Morris was the attending and Doctor Baren was the resident. That wouldn't be helpful, though, because the docs don't do scans on their own."

"How do you store imaging studies like C.T.s?" Elise wondered.

"On optical disk since nineteen ninety, before that, on tapes, " explained Charlie. "Of course, we have hard copies in the file room as well."

"So if someone wanted a copy of a C.T. study, it isn't duplicated like radiographs? A new set of films is made off of the disk or tape?" Elise asked. To obtain her copy, she had informally asked one of the techs to duplicate the films in Mr. Weber's folder, again in order to bypass mean old Sister Margaret Mary.

"Yeah," he confirmed.

"Could it be altered?" Eric asked.

"I don't think so," Charlie replied hesitantly.

"Could we take a look at the disk copy of this C.T., please?"

Elise handed Charlie the films. He disappeared into the file room and returned with a disk several minutes later. He inserted it into the drive in the C.T. scanner and punched in numbers. When the images came up on the screen, Charlie's face registered his surprise.

Mr. Weber's disk C.T. scan showed some shrinkage of the brain as would be expected of an elderly person, but there was no evidence of blood or any other pathology.

"These are totally different studies, I don't understand. And look, the tech number is one-sixteen on this set of films," Charlie noted.

"Portable x-ray in E.R., portable chest in E.R.," boomed the intercom. Elise cringed. She hated when people referred to the emergency department as the "E.R.".

"Charlie, you're a doll! Do you think I could have a copy of these films, please?" she requested sweetly.

"No problem," he said as he punched buttons on the computer keyboard. "They'll come out over there."

"Thanks a million. Have a great rest of your shift. See you soon," Elise thanked him as he left the department to take the portable chest x-ray in the E.D.

"The plot thickens. Someone wanted to deliberately make us think your grandfather had a massive brain hemorrhage so we would find his death unremarkable," Elise said excitedly.

Eric's face looked ashen and he was silent. They backtracked their steps to return to the car. "Could you take me home?" she requested.


Eric tried not to show his disappointment as he started the car. He was really starting to enjoy the vivacious doctor's company. When they got to Elise's apartment and he stopped in front, Elise looked perplexed.

"What are you doing? Aren't you coming in? We still have work to do."

Eric's countenance brightened as he realized she wasn't ending their date early. He found a superb parking spot half a block away and they hurried upstairs.

Elise flicked on the lights and Eric looked around as she excused herself to go to the kitchen. He liked her taste in decorating; her apartment was furnished in contemporary style and was bright and airy. He marveled at how neat it was and then realized she probably didn't spend enough time at home to make a mess. As he reached down to stroke the purring cat nuzzling his legs, he appreciatively noted the absence of cat odor. Eric moved closer to the entertainment center and examined her knick-knacks and pictures. *This woman is obviously her sister*, he thought. *I wonder who this handsome man is?*

Elise seemed to read his mind as she said, "My brother, Don, and my sister, Shelly. I have to tell you, Eric, I'm totally impressed that my cat is nuzzling up to you. Most people never even know he exists. He's pretty skittish."

She handed him a mug of hot chocolate with a dollop of whipped cream and a smattering of cinnamon on top and continued the photographic tour as she pointed out her parents, grandmother, Janice, and several other friends.

After Eric had made the pictorial acquaintance of her loved ones, Elise walked over to a small table and withdrew some films from a folder. "This is the scan I told you about. It's supposedly of a John Babcock, Jr. who was born in nineteen twenty-four, done in nineteen ninety-three, and notice right here? The tech who performed the scan, numero fifty-eight," she said triumphantly.

"What exactly do you think that means?" Eric asked.

"I think tech fifty-eight *did* do the scan. I think she did it of Mister Babcock years ago. Then, I think someone took Mister Babcock's record and changed it so this scan would appear to be your grandfather's. They must have inputted false information to eliminate the true identity and then printed out the hard copies we saw. I just knew there was no way your grandfather could have had such a massive and fatal stroke without more physical signs. So we are left with more questions. How did he really die, why was his C.T. faked and by whom?"

"I really have no clue. The Jewish religion is not keen on autopsies, but maybe if we go to the police, they could arrange it."

Elise thought to herself how odd it would be for Eric to suggest involving law enforcement if he were the culprit.

"Let's not involve the police yet. You know, the one weird thing I recall is Sid Shulman being in the E.D. It isn't every day that the president of the hospital comes down to visit us. In fact, I've never seen him down there before," Elise noted aloud.

"Elise, my grandfather was pretty tight with the upper echelon of C.G.H. Sid and PopPop used to socialize at their posh country club. When Grandma was sick, Sid visited her a lot. It wouldn't surprise me if he had stopped down to the emergency department when she was admitted. Frankly, I would have been more surprised if Sid hadn't come down when PopPop was in the E.R.," Eric countered.

"Just the same, I wonder just how bad C.G.H.'s finances are doing? There has been a lot of rumbling going on about H.M.O.s effectively closing down local hospitals who are competition. Maybe C.G.H. is a lot more desperate than they are letting on, " Elise surmised. Her eyes narrowed suspiciously.

"But PopPop didn't leave a lot of money," Eric pointed out.

"Good point."

Elise paused for a moment and thought. "Wait, I thought you said your grandfather wasn't really sharing that information. Maybe someone thought there was a lot more money at stake than there was. Would he have shared his financial situation with Doctor Shulman?" Elise asked.

"No way! That would have been too embarrassing," Eric answered.

"When he was practicing, Sid Shulman was a neurologist. He certainly would have the ability to cause your grandfather's death and find a way to manipulate the C.T. to make it look legit," Elise hypothesized. "You said your grandfather's estate wasn't settled yet? When do you think it will be? When were you planning on making his bequest?"

"Actually, that should be soon. Our lawyer told me everything was almost wrapped up."

"Cool. We'll have to figure out a way to test Sid. I want to know if he killed your grandfather," Elise said.

"Sid?! That's insane! There's just no way! And even if it were true, how are we going to prove something farfetched like that?! We're going to need to get the police involved," Eric reiterated.

"I have a better idea. We'll figure it out ourselves. Tomorrow. Tonight, I have something else in mind," Elise said mischievously.

She reached over and removed the steaming mug from Eric's hand.

*What else should I have expected from an assertive woman doctor?* he thought as he smiled and willingly allowed himself to be kissed. *I have some ideas of my own*, he thought as he caressed her auburn hair and kissed her full lips right back.

# CHAPTER 11

"I'd love to," Elise answered. *He invited me for dinner at his place! I can't seem to stop thinking about him. We've just been having so much fun together. If it weren't for this awful business about his grandfather, things would be perfect!* "Eight o'clock it is."

She lifted herself out of the couch and refilled her coffee mug. As Elise exited the staff lounge, she greeted Kathy as she passed. "We haven't had a patient together yet today. I didn't even know you were working today."

"Are you avoiding me?" Kathy asked playfully.

"Elise, can I present a patient, please?" asked the medical student, Stacey Buch, as she approached.

"Sure, what have you got?" Elise said.

"This is a twenty-six year old black female with a history of schizophrenia and hypertension who awoke this morning with onset of right sided facial weakness and slurred speech. She gets a monthly shot of Prolixin, takes Cogentin, and Vasotec. Her physical examination reveals some early hypertensive changes in her fundi, and a right-sided facial droop. Her right side may be slightly weaker, but reflexes are okay. I'd like to get some baseline labs and do a C.T. scan," she concluded.

*Waste of labs, but interns have to learn that for themselves by ordering enough negative tests.* "Sounds reasonable, I'll see her in a while."

The board was a mess. Patients had been flowing in all day in the pre-holiday rush. Elise signed her initials to a '*R. ear pain*' and a '*wrist pain*' to try to expedite things. She quickly dispatched the sixty-two year old woman with wrist pain to Radiology to see how badly displaced her broken wrist was. Winter was brutal on the elderly - if it was icy outside, it would be broken wrist and hip day inside.

Elise entered Room Eleven, the ear, nose, and throat room, and was surprised to see an adult. The complaint of '*ear pain*' usually translated to an ear infection in a child.

"Miss Coffey, what seems to be the problem?" Elise asked.

"My ear hurts," the woman answered with a wince. She held her head tipped to the right with her hand over her ear.

"Let me take a peek," the doctor said as she bent down to peer in the woman's ear with her otoscope. "Eeeeew!" she yelped.

"What?!" exclaimed the patient anxiously.

*Oh, I just HATE when they say, "my ear hurts," when they mean, "there's something in my ear,"* Elise thought with annoyance.

"You seem to have a cockroach in your ear, dear. I'll need to remove it*." Gross, I hate doing this!* Elise thought silently, her face only partially disguising her repulsion.

"Oh, that's why it's so noisy, too," observed the suffering woman. "I know people who sleep with cotton in their ears. Me, too, from now on," she vowed.

Elise poured some medicine in the woman's ear to kill the invading insect and then carefully pulled out the readily accessible body parts. She flushed the ear out with saline to remove the last remnants and then reexamined the ear to see if there had been any damage. The doctor prescribed some ear drops for the superficial scratches which had resulted, either from the bug or the therapy. Ms. Coffey was slightly disgusted, but pleased with her prompt treatment and signed her discharge papers willingly.

She tipped her head from side to side.

"Praise the Lord, it's quiet again!" she said with a smile as she left the examining room, to no one in particular.

As the satisfied customer exited through the glass sliding doors, she was almost plowed down by the paramedics exploding through the doors from the other direction.

Megan Larson, EMT-P, excitedly called for help and was instructed to go into Room Three.

"We got him from a restaurant in Chinatown. We were picking up lunch, so we were right there. Since we were only a few minutes out, we scooped and ran. I'm sorry we didn't have time to call in," she apologized.

"What have you got?" Elise asked urgently.

"I'm not sure. His friends said he was eating some dim sum and he started grabbing at his throat and choking," the paramedic responded as the group lifted the sheet under the patient and transferred him to the hospital gurney on the count of three. "We tried a Heimlich maneuver but nothing happened. We put him on a non-rebreather and bolted."

Mr. Chinese-food looked bad! His face was a dusky gray-purple, his lips and eyes were swollen, and his thrashing about was getting less active by the moment. The nurses were cutting off his expensive double-breasted Armani suit and applying monitor leads to reveal a rapid heart rate.

"His BP is sixty by doppler," Kathy informed Elise.

"Hook him back up to the oxygen at fifteen liters per minute and get me the intubation tray," ordered Elise as she leaned over to listen to the patient's lungs. She heard very little air movement, and what little she did hear sounded wheezy.

"I think maybe he's having an allergic reaction," Elise explained aloud. "Give him one amp of epi I.V., two hundred fifty milligrams of Solumedrol and fifty of Benadryl I.V. *STAT*!"

Elise grabbed the intubation tray and removed the materials she would need. She opened an 8.0 endotracheal tube, checked the balloon and slathered sterile water-based lubricant on the tip. She checked the laryngoscope light. She rummaged around for a stylet and inserted it in her tube when she found it.

Fortunately, within the amount of time it took Elise to prepare for intubation, Mr. Chinese-food's face pinked up and his breathing became more rhythmical and less labored. Elise hesitated to place her tube, and she was inordinately pleased that the mere threat of it had fixed the patient! Ten minutes later he was able to speak in short phrases.

"Allergic to shrimp."

"Well, why did you order something with shrimp in it?" Ann, who had pushed the medications, asked incredulously.

"Didn't. Maybe they fried my food in the same oil with shrimp. I thought I was a goner," he somberly mused.

"Not today, sir," Elise said as she squeezed his hand and started out of the room. "I'm thinking you need to take an epi-pen with you when you go out for Chinese."

"Doctor!" the patient entreated.

"Yes?" she asked as she stopped at the threshold.

"Thank you very much."

"You're very welcome," she said cheerfully. It always made her day to have someone express a little gratitude instead of complaints.


As she left the room, she noticed Jenifer Howard, the nurse supervisor for the emergency department. She veered towards her casually.

"Hi, Jen, how are you?" Elise asked.

"I'm fine, Elise. How is being chief resident going? Do you have any resident beefs you want to tell me about? Everyone else has been complaining today," Jen said. She was tall and big-boned with a plain face and a warm heart. She was an excellent administrator because she really listened and was able to identify what was really on peoples' minds.

"No complaints today, but can I ask you something?" Elise said.

"Of course," Jen answered.

"Have you heard anything concrete about the hospital being in trouble financially?" Elise explored.

"Did you attend Sid Shulman's hospital-wide forum?" Jen asked.

Elise nodded affirmatively.

"Well, you remember way back when Humana took over Michael Reese? We thought then that the H.M.O.s were intercalating themselves in the area. Now Medcare Healthnet is vying for several other hospitals and physician practices," she started and then continued when Elise nodded. "C.G.H. is trying to position itself favorably in the Chicago area. Marketing is expensive as is opening centers of excellence to attract customers. I've heard rumors that the hospital is in need of a capital bolus, if you know what I mean. However, I haven't heard that our jobs or the institution are really in immediate jeopardy."

Elise thanked Jen for the information. She wondered if this added credence to the notion that Sid could have arranged for Mr. Weber's demise just for the money.

She looked at her watch. *Speaking of suspects...* Elise turned to the attending who was dawdling by the clerk's desk.

"I need to run to my office for a minute. My patients are all on autopilot. Page me if you need me."

She informed the charge nurse that she was leaving the department and would be reachable by pager. Elise trotted down the corridor and hung a quick left. She greeted two surgical residents in the stairwell. In anticipation, she bounded up the steps two at a time. When she reached the second floor, she exited and walked through the double glass doors into the department offices.

She walked past the conference room quickly. The chief resident's room next to it was vacant and Elise exhaled a sigh of relief. She closed the door and sat down at the desk. The clock radio blinked three-fifteen p.m.

Referring to the telephone number in the middle of the business card she held in her hand, she cleared her throat and dialed cautiously.

"Yes, hello. Is this the secretary for Mister Eric Weber?" Elise asked in a husky voice.

"Yes, it is. I'm sorry, Mister Weber is not in. He is in a meeting until four. Would you like to leave a message?" replied his secretary professionally.

"No, actually, it's you I'd like to talk to, Miss..." Elise fished for her name.

"Miss Felter. To whom am I speaking?" Ms. Felter inquired curiously.

"My name is Denise Dubois. I'm a reporter for the Chicago Tribune. You are familiar with the Trib, I presume?" Elise fibbed smoothly and engagingly.

The secretary chortled.

Elise continued, "We are doing a story on some of the most eligible bachelors in the metro Chicago area and we were given Mister Weber's name. Can I assume we can have this conversation confidentially?"

"Oh, yes!" confirmed the young woman on the other end of the line. "What did you need to know?"

Elise ran through demographics and facts which she already knew and wanted to confirm. She also wanted her cover to seem plausible.

"One of the recurring themes we have seen in these most desirable men is familial harmony. Does Mister Weber fit that profile? Does he get along with his family?" Elise asked.

"Actually, it's quite sad. Mister Weber's parents were killed many years ago and in August, his only living relative, his grandfather, passed away. They usually got along well," Ms. Felter stated.

Elise picked up on it immediately. "Were they not getting along before his grandfather died?"

"I had heard some arguing about a woman, but I know Mister Weber really loved his grandfather," defended the secretary.

"Speaking of women, does Mister Weber have anyone special in his life right now?" Elise questioned.

"I believe he had recently started seeing someone, but I'm not sure how serious things are. It must not have been her birthday yet; he hasn't sent me out to buy her a last minute present," Ms. Felter said and the women shared a knowing chuckle. "That won't affect your mentioning him in the article, will it?" asked the administrative assistant anxiously.

"I doubt it. How long has it been since he was seriously romantically involved with someone?" delved Elise.

"Hmmm, he had been dating an accountant for about a year, but she broke it off last summer. I think she was too insecure to accept Mister Weber's close friendship with that same woman Eric's grandfather disapproved of. I suppose *that* might have developed into something, but she tragically died," the secretary speculated.

"One last thing, Miss Felter. Does Mister Weber have a tendency to buy excessive gifts for his girlfriends, does he spend a lot of money trying to impress and woo them?" Elise wanted to further explore the financial motive.

"Mister Weber is very generous, but not outrageous. He is a very nice person, and I think he wins his women by his intelligence, warmth, and wit, not by buying their affections," Ms. Felter rebuffed her soundly.

Elise concluded her bogus interview and hung up. On her way back to the department, she considered the information she had received. Reluctantly, thoughts of Eric and intrigue were relegated to the back of her mind as she refocused on the E.D..


Her next patient was Wendy Dayton, a thin twenty-eight year old blonde engineer. Her chief complaint read, *I fell through the ceiling*.

Elise took one look at Wendy and her own heart started racing. The patient was lying very still on the cart and looked ghostly pale. Her pulse was thready and at a rate of 136. Elise glanced at the triage note again and was surprised to see the initial vital signs of heart rate -98, blood pressure-104/56, and respirations of 20. And it had been written up two hours previously!

Elise stuck her head outside the curtain of Room Six and calmly, but urgently, asked for some nursing assistance. When Ann came in, Elise asked her to repeat vital signs, hook the young woman up to a monitor, and start two large intravenous lines with lactated ringer's solution infusing wide open. They checked the pulse oximeter which showed an oxygen saturation of ninety-two percent. Elise grabbed some tubing for oxygen and hooked one end up to the wall and the other end to Ms. Dayton's nose.

"Miss Dayton, what exactly were you doing that made you come in tonight?" Elise inquired.

"I recently bought a two flat downtown and I am renovating it. I was up in the attic," she paused to catch her breath, " and fell through the floor."

"How many feet did you fall? How did you land?" Elise tried to ascertain in order to anticipate injuries. Elise mentally ran through it as she waited for the answer. *If she landed on her feet, the likely injuries would be fractures of the heels or lower spine, and injury to the kidneys. If she landed on her back, she could have broken her neck or spine. If she landed on her shoulder...*

"No, I didn't fall through the floor. I fell *into* the floor. I got caught at the waist. God, my chest hurts!" Ms. Dayton winced. She was clutching her left chest.

Elise lifted up the patient's hospital gown and, over the lower part of the side of her ribcage on the left, noted a large angry, purple bruise with some superficial abrasion overlying it. There was no active bleeding, but Elise recognized that she could easily have broken ribs.

"Ann, please get a portable chest x-ray, a blood gas, a C.B.C., basic metabolic profile, PT/PTT, and a type and screen. Oh, yeah, and a urine dip and pregnancy test," the resident listed. She placed her stethoscope in her ears and instructed Ms. Dayton to take deep breaths in and out.

"Miss Dayton, I think you may have a collapsed lung here which is causing your oxygen to be low. You probably broke some ribs and very well may have bleeding in your chest which is causing you to have a rapid heart rate."

Elise continued her physical examination. When she got to the abdominal examination, she was alarmed to see how tender Wendy was in the abdomen below the ribcage. Her muscles resisted palpation and Elise realized that she had underestimated the severity of the patient's injuries.

"Oh, Ann, please change that type and screen to a type and crossmatch for six units. And change the B.M.P. to a comprehensive panel and add amylase to the bloods. Also, we'll need an N.G. tube and a Foley. Maybe we should move Miss Dayton into Room One,"

Elise suggested firmly. "Miss Dayton, is there anyone here with you?"

"My fiancé," she gasped.

"Let's bring him in after we move you into the other room and I'll explain what is going on." Elise nodded to Ann that she could move the patient out into the trauma resuscitation room.

Elise called Joel and gave him her impression, "I think she has fractured ribs, a pneumo or hemothorax, or both, and I'm worried that she caught her spleen too. She is hemodynamically unstable but I'm giving her fluids. If we can stabilize her, I'll get a C.T. scan of the abdomen. Otherwise, you guys need to do a peritoneal lavage and may be going to the O.R. blind."

Elise glanced at the panel of monitors as she walked toward the x-ray viewboard. A rapid rhythm caught her eye. At first she thought it was Ms. Dayton, but it was the monitor reading from Room Four. The rate was two-hundred ten, which caused Elise to divert past the flow board.

No one had signed up for the patient in Room Four, so Elise picked up the chart and went in. She saw a seven-year-old girl, smiling and pointing out the Tiny Toons characters on her patient gown to her dad.

"Hi, Sara," she started. "I'm Doctor Silver. Who is that?"

"Baby Bugs," answered the little girl. She grinned what would have been a toothy grin, had she not been missing her front two teeth, and Elise had to laugh.

"Gee, Sara, what do you want for Christmas?" she asked.

The reference went over the little girl's head and she began a laundry list of toys that Elise had never heard of.

"Now, why are you here tonight?" Elise asked.

"My stomach was beating fast," she declared very seriously.

Elise had to laugh again.

"Does anything hurt? Are you having trouble breathing?" she inquired.

"Nope," answered the little patient.

Elise gathered more information from Sara's parents as the P.C.T., Jack, hooked the little girl up to the E.K.G. machine and ran off a twelve lead E.K.G.. Elise looked it over and asked Jack to send a nurse in.

"Tell her to bring some Adenocard. Also, ask the intern to come in, too," Elise suggested. She turned to Mr. and Mrs. Grosser, "Sara is having an abnormal heartbeat called supraventricular tachycardia, or S.V.T. for short. Has she ever had this before?"

"She may have, but we never brought her to the hospital for it. It just went away and we didn't think much of it. I feel just awful now," answered her mother, wringing her hands. "Is it dangerous?"

"She's young and healthy and tolerating the rapid rate just fine. We'll give her medicine to stop it. Who is her regular doctor?"

"Doctor Romano. We called him and he told us to come in to the emergency room," Mr. Grosser said.

Elise explained to the intern and medical student that she was going to try several things to see if they could stop the dysrhythmia while they waited for the nurse to bring in the medicine. First she had Sara bear down like she had to have a bowel movement. No success. Then she tried gagging the little patient with a tongue depressor. She succeeded in annoying Sara, but her heart rate stayed in the two hundreds range. She even stuck a washcloth with ice on Sara's face to try to evoke the diving reflex. The senior resident explained to her audience that this was an evolutionary response to being immersed in cold water. It slowed down the person's system to try to save his life in the event of near drowning. Adults usually did not respond to this, but children often did.

"Well, none of the vagal maneuvers stopped the S.V.T. What should we give now?" Elise asked Gregory Jackson, the intern.

"Adenosine," he answered swiftly.

Elise smiled. "You know, Greg, in the olden days they used Verapamil. But now the drug of choice is adenosine. It's a compound found naturally in the body and often works. It is quite rapid in onset and harmless if you've mistaken ventricular tachycardia for S.V.T. It can be quite impressive."

And with that, Elise instructed Nicole to give the fifty-six pound girl two and a half milligrams of adenosine.

"Start the strip running," she told Steven as the nurse meticulously drew up the proper dosage of medicine in a syringe.

"I don't want another shot," wailed Sara.

They explained it was going into her intravenous line, and she wouldn't feel any shot. Sara settled down sensibly and waited to see what would happen.

Within seconds of the medicine being injected into the I.V. line, Sara scrunched up her face and said, "I feel funny."

Everyone's attention was on the monitor and they got to watch Sara's heart stop for a few seconds before it started up again at a normal rate. Sara confirmed that she felt much better.

She pulled up her gown over her head and pointed, "Look, my stomach isn't beating anymore!"

Everyone present laughed. Her mother leaned down and gave her a big hug and kiss.

"We'll observe her for a while and I'm going to give Doctor Romano a call. Sara may need further tests, but she probably doesn't need to stay in the hospital tonight," Elise reassured the family.


As they walked out together, Greg said, "Doc Tony is my family doctor, too. He's quite something. Do you know about his medication donation program?"

Elise replied in the negative and Greg explained, "You know he has a huge patient base. He's one of the last dinosaurs who still makes house calls, hard as that is to believe. Anyway, when one of his patients passes away, he gets permission from the family to collect the person's left over medications. He then donates them in the patient's name to an organization that distributes meds to poor people who can't afford to buy the medications they need. Some of the new AIDS medicines and antibiotics are quite exorbitant."

"What a humanitarian thing to do," Elise agreed.


Eventually the department came under control. Her lady did have a broken wrist and the orthopedics resident came down to splint it. Stacey came to tell Elise that her patient, Ms. Crutchfield, had returned from C.T. scan. They walked into the room together.

Elise took one look at the patient on the cart and something seemed wrong, yet familiar. The woman's face appeared contorted, but she was sitting upright, not slouching.

"Missus Crutchfield, I'm Doctor Silver. Do you have a headache?"

"No," she replied.

"Has this ever happened to you before?"

"Yeah," Ms. Crutchfield said.

"When you don't take your Cogentin?" asked Elise.

"I din't have no money to fill my perscripshun," slurred the patient.

Elise demonstrated hand grasps to the intern and they discovered the minimal right-sided weakness was secondary to the patient being left-handed.

"The pronator drift test is the most sensitive for subtle weakness," Elise explained as she had the patient hold her arms straight out in front of her with her eyes closed. The arms stayed in place, and the test did not reveal any problem.

"We'll get you fixed up in a jiffy. Be sure to get your prescription filled or this can happen again," Elise admonished.

The physicians left the room and Elise gave the primary nurse an order to administer a shot of Cogentin to the patient.

"That was a classic dystonic reaction. Only her face and tongue were involved and there was significant muscle spasm. All the symptoms did not fit together for a classic stroke pattern - no limb involvement, normal reflexes. Often it is a good idea to ask the patient what he thinks is wrong; they are often correct."

*A rather expensive lesson to learn*, Elise thought. *I could have prevented it had I seen the patient before she went to C.T.* However, in emergency medicine, the first rule is '*Rule out life threats.*' In other words, make sure a patient isn't having any serious problem, before you assume they just have something minor. This was the main difference between emergency medicine and other fields of medicine. A child with a fever had pneumonia or meningitis until proven otherwise; chest pain was a heart attack or an aortic dissection or lung pathology until all appropriate tests revealed it to be merely a muscle strain. And when the department is a chaotic mess, the junior residents and students often have to manage patients until a more senior doctor can free him (or her)self up to supervise and apply years of experience to more accurately recognize disease processes foregoing elaborate, and often unnecessary, testing.

But the thing that really struck Elise was how similar the presentation was to Eric's grandfather. *Maybe that explains why the symptoms didn't add up. But he wasn't on any medication that could cause a dystonic reaction. Or was he? Not according to his records*, she recalled. *Was there anything in his system?* Unless they exhumed his body, there was no way of knowing because no autopsy had been performed. *Wait a minute, or was there?*

Ignoring the building mound of charts in the to-be-seen rack, Elise went to her briefcase and shuffled through the papers until she located her xeroxed copy of Mr. Weber's chart. She thumbed through the pages and found what she was looking for. Eric had filled out the niclodipine study data entry sheet for his grandfather. There was a code number on the top which corresponded to the tubes of blood which had been drawn from the patient. *I hope they haven't tossed the blood!* she thought.

"Leaving the department," Elise sang as she jogged out the side door to make her way to the laboratory department.

She entered the R.I.A. section, the area where samples were evaluated to quantify levels of particular drugs or hormones. She found a diminutive Filipino technician and explained that the patient in question had died and she wanted to retrieve his blood.

"Oh, Doctah, I don't know if I can find old blood."

"Please check for me," Elise implored.

The lab tech scrutinized the death certificate and Elise's I.D. badge to satisfy herself that this activity was kosher. She then swung open the heavy metal door of the huge walk-in refrigerator and disappeared. Each second was an eternity. Elise held her breath and crossed her fingers. Finally, the small technician emerged and handed Elise two blood-filled red-topped test tubes labeled with the appropriate code number. Since the patient had expired, the tests had never been run, but, luckily, the samples had also not been discarded.

When she returned to the E.D., Elise referred to her electronic telephone book and dialed Mark's work number.

"Medical examiner's office, may I help you?" answered the receptionist.

"Yes, I'd like to speak to Doctor Procino, please. This is Doctor Silver calling."

After a few interminable moments of Muzak, Mark picked up the line.

"Hey, stranger, long time no hear!"

"Mark, what are you doing for lunch tomorrow?" Elise asked.

"No plans. What did you have in mind?" he replied.

"I'd love to take you out. You pick the place, I'll pay."

"Sounds like a good deal to me. Come by around noon," he suggested.

"Great. Mark?"

"Yeah?"

"Wear your Drakkar Noir," Elise recommended.

Mark laughed and they hung up.


Joel grabbed Elise as she left the lounge. "You were right. She ruptured her spleen. Her hematocrit is twenty-four now after hydration. We're taking her to the O.R. soon. What a bizarre mechanism of injury. Think we could do a case report for the Journal of Weird Stories and Wild Mechanisms?!"

"Sure, only if I get second author!" Elise replied jokingly.

# CHAPTER 12

The remainder of Elise's shift was uneventful, and she miraculously got out on time. She freshened up in the ladies' room and drove to Eric's house. She was both excited and nervous about going to his place for the first time. Eric lived in a nice section of Lincoln Park where there were many older single family homes and duplexes. She referred to her Post-it and glanced up, looking for number *forty-nine*. His building was a large brownstone and it was obviously well kept. There were flower boxes lining the stairway, currently devoid of flowers and filled with snow. Elise noted light in several windows. It looked warm and welcoming.

She rang the doorbell and he buzzed her in. She mounted the inside steps and Eric opened the inner door. A delicious aroma met her nose as Eric took her coat. He ushered her into the living room and handed her a glass of chilled Sauvignon Blanc.

"I'd love the fifty cent tour if you are offering," she said.

"Dinner will be ready in about fifteen minutes. Step this way," he replied.

Eric escorted her around the four-bedroom house. Elise was duly impressed with the styling and cleanliness of his home. Eric lived in the master bedroom on the second floor and it was attractively decorated and neat. The other bedrooms on that floor were set up as an office and a workout room.

"I have to confess that I have a woman come in once a week to clean," he admitted. "I'm pretty lucky that I have no mortgage. PopPop and Grandma bought this house forty years ago. It has probably appreciated several hundred-fold in value."

Eric was amazed at how lovely the young physician looked after a hard day at work. He sat her down in an oversized armchair in the living room by a roaring fire and rubbed her neck.

"Mmmm, my trapezius is so tight," Elise murmured.

"Yeah, so are your neck muscles." They laughed. Elise tipped her head back and welcomed Eric's soft lips. He pulled away only reluctantly.

"Hey, I've slaved over a hot stove all day. If you distract me, my birds will burn," and with that he returned to the kitchen to put the finishing touches on dinner.

Elise excused herself and entered the first floor bathroom. It was next to the bedroom which had apparently been Jefferey Weber's room. After she washed her hands, she surreptitiously opened the medicine cabinet. It was still stocked and she eyed the medication bottles. *Vasotec, 5 mg once a day, Coumadin, 1/2 tablet and 1 full tablet on alternating days, Dyazide once a day*, she read the labels. The date on the bottles was *August 21, 2000* and there were two refills left. Elise opened the bottles and examined the pills inside. The Coumadin and Dyazide had their names on them, but Elise could not positively identify the pills in the Vasotec container. She removed a pill and placed it in her pocket. There was also some Tylenol and Maalox, shaving apparatus, and cologne. Then she saw it. Back in the corner, barely noticeable, almost completely hidden behind a Pepto-Bismol bottle, was a small bottle with a Clark-Davies logo and no label. In it she found four identical pills with which she was unfamiliar. She slipped one of those into her pocket as well and returned to the living room.

Elise looked around the room. On the wall, there was a thirty-two inch TV in the center of an expensive looking entertainment center and a pretty impressive array of sound equipment flanking it. There was a soft leather sofa next to her chair and the coffee table had several piles of books and decorative glass paperweights strategically arranged. The flickering emanating from the warm fire was hypnotic. On the end table next to her, she noted a festive invitation to a New Year's Eve party. She nosily glanced inside and read the flowery calligraphy. She was surprised to see it was from Dr. Romano.

"I didn't realize Doctor Romano lived so close to you," she remarked as she recognized the address was only a few numbers away from Eric's.

"Yeah, I house sit for him sometimes when he goes on vacation. Did you hear about him?" he called back from the kitchen.

"No, what?" she replied curiously.

"Remember about four months ago there was a lottery worth thirty-eight million dollars and it went to a single winner?" he asked.

"Oh, yeah. My friend, Janice, told me he was the winner."

"Yes, he was. I guess he figures he can splurge a little on a major holiday bash."

"Didn't his wife pass away very recently?"

"What a euphemism. Linda didn't pass away; she killed herself," Eric said almost bitterly.

"Did you know her well too?" Elise questioned.

"We were," Elise noted a slight hesitation, "good friends. Doc Tony and Linda met about three years ago. He was older by a lot. He picked her up at the hospital when she was an idealistic resident who got all moony that such a distinguished and important attending physician would be interested in her. They had a whirlwind courtship and got married. Linda was somewhat of a computer nerd in college and I don't think she had many relationships before Doc Tony."

"Why do you think she killed herself, Eric?" Elise asked curiously.

"Linda had been depressed for a while. It's not common knowledge, but Doc Tony was...is, I guess, a gambler. She confided in me that they were having some financial troubles and she was picking up extra work at another hospital for the cash. I think she resented having to work extra because she wanted to start a family. She was kind of bummed that she wasn't pregnant yet and then things started going sour in their relationship," he answered.

Elise detected a strange tone in Eric's voice.

"Did you care for Linda?" she asked hesitantly, not sure if she wanted to hear the answer.

"Doc Tony was good friends with my grandfather, probably since I was a kid. I met Linda through them and she helped me set up my computer system. We spent a lot of time together. Don't tell your brother, the cop, but she even gave me some bootleg software."

Elise chuckled. She was still waiting for an answer to her question.

"Yes, I cared for her. She really did have a beautiful soul. If she wasn't already married, we probably would have had a much deeper relationship. I don't want to sound conceited and I don't want to talk ill of the dead, but I think Linda started having some romantic feelings for me. My grandfather noticed and, of course, he didn't approve because she wasn't Jewish. But I wouldn't get involved with a married woman anyway. It's not moral," he said and then took a deep swig of his wine. "What I am really sorry about is I didn't recognize how depressed she really was. I didn't have a clue that she was going to kill herself. And I can't say that I approve of the length of his mourning, she's barely cold in the grave."

"I'm sorry, Eric. You shouldn't feel guilty about it. There really wasn't anything you could do."

Elise paused and tried to change the subject. "Hey, do you ever daydream about what you would do if you won the lottery?"

"Not really, but my grandfather used to all the time. Even when he was wealthy, he was still very frugal. He and Grandma didn't go on many fun vacations. They thought there would always be tomorrow, you know? Well, Grandma died and there wasn't tomorrow after all. Then he lost his money. There were a lot of things he had put off that he wished he had done. He worried about me, too, not that he needed to. I have a great job which pays well, and, frankly, money isn't everything. But PopPop used to play the lottery religiously. Every Wednesday and Saturday, the same numbers. PopPop and Grandma's birthdays, my father and my birthdays, our address, and the number sixteen because he used to say there were always two consecutive numbers. Actually, it's kind of ironic. Doc Tony was more of a big-time gambler. He used to go to Las Vegas a lot. Obviously he wasn't very good at it either.

You wouldn't think the state lottery would have been exciting enough for his taste."


A frantic ding from the kitchen signaled Eric that his Cornish hens were done resting and were ready to be carved. He went back into the kitchen to finish, rebuffing Elise's offers to help.

"Dinner is served!"

Eric arranged serving dishes on the dining room table which had a beautiful bouquet of flowers and two peach scented tapered candles in crystal candlesticks. He served her hens with an orange glaze, wild rice pilaf, steamed broccoli with a subtle lemon sauce, followed by a decadent dessert of raspberry mousse with homemade whipped cream.

"So what would you do if *you* won the lottery?" Eric asked.

Elise smiled.

"First of all, I never take the initiative to buy my own tickets. I'll go in on a pool at work, but I would never remember to get my own ticket. So, I don't figure I would ever end up with that much money. But, just for the sake of discussion, what would I do if I won the lottery? I think I might keep working a few shifts a month, because I really do love practicing medicine. But I would do a lot more traveling. I would take some courses like a pottery course and a photography course. I'd pay off my student loans. I'd give my parents some money. I guess I really don't have any wild aspirations," she answered.

It was the best home cooked meal Elise had enjoyed in a long time. She admitted that domesticity was not her strong suit and Eric told her he loved to cook.

"Well, Eric, if I win the lottery, I'll buy you unlimited groceries, and you can cook for me all the time," Elise declared.

Eric lifted his wineglass and clinked hers.

"It's a deal!" he said.

# CHAPTER 13

Elise outlined the problem to Mark as they ate at Rosebud the next afternoon.

"So do you think you could do a comprehensive tox screen on this blood?" she asked.

"It's been properly stored. I don't see why not. What exactly are you looking for?" the pathologist inquired as he removed a small notepad from his pocket to take notes.

"A drug which could cause a dystonic reaction to mimic stroke symptoms," Elise answered.

"What medications was he on regularly?"

Elise named the drugs and their dosages. Mark jotted the information down.

"Well, I'll run some standard screens and if I need to, I can look for more specific and unusual drugs," Mark offered.

"Great!" Elise said as she paid the bill and went back to his office with him. "Oh, by the way, could you check something on the Identidex for me?"

Elise referred to a computerized service which could identify an unknown pill from its markings.

Mark booted up his computer and asked, "What does it say?"

Elise removed the small oddly shaped white pill from a plastic baggie and read off the markings: *MSD 712*. Mark typed it in and confirmed that this was, indeed, Vasotec, five milligrams.

"How about the other one?" he said as he motioned to the second pill in the baggie.

Elise manipulated the round, dark yellow pill in her fingers until the letters and numbers came into view. "C dash D, number five sixty-six," she read.

He typed in the data on the keyboard and waited for the list to come up. "That is Clark-Davies' form of prochlorperazine, twenty-five mg. Antiemezine is the trade name."

Elise inhaled sharply. Prochlorperazine was a medication used to prevent vomiting, but the fact which caught her attention was it could have an undesirable side effect of causing a dystonic reaction. Now what was this medication doing in PopPop's medicine chest?

"Please check and see if this was in Mister Weber's system too, could you?"

He marked this down as well. "Sure, when do you need the results?" the assistant medical examiner asked his friend.

"As soon as possible!" Elise kissed him on the cheek and said, "You're a love!" She grinned and teased as she paused in the doorway, "And you smell good, too!"


Elise drove back to C.G.H. deep in thought. *Could I be wrong about Eric?* She remembered how wonderful it felt to have his arms around her, to be kissed and cuddled. *How could someone like that calculatingly murder his only living relative? And what would his motive have been? Was he really having money trouble, but not mentioning it? Did it have something to do with his relationship with Linda? It just can't be!* she decided.


As Elise entered the E.D., Nancy immediately sought her attention. "Hurry up, put away your coat and get your equipment! The patient in Room Eight needs you desperately!"

Elise stepped into the lounge and retrieved her lab coat off a hook on the back of the door. She grabbed her stethoscope out of her briefcase. The resident didn't notice the nurses and clerk tittering and giggling as she strolled into the room.

She gasped when she saw the figure lying on the cart. Her wide green eyes scanned his supine form. He was at least six and a half feet tall, immobilized on a backboard with towels taped on either side of his head to prevent movement of his neck. He was dark skinned and his forehead was enormous and irregularly shaped. He had a severe beard and his hair was long and unruly. He was attired in a standard Klingon military uniform, complete with phaser. The beautiful physician jumped when the man started to growl. The growl crescendoed to a howl and Elise referred to his chart.

The nurses could no longer contain themselves and they burst out laughing. It was well known in the department that Elise was a Star Trek fanatic and this patient had been hand selected especially for her.

As Elise read the triage note and listened to Mr. Khan's explanation, it became clear. There was a Star Trek convention being held at the Hyatt close to Chicago General Hospital. During an exhibition of the Klingon equivalent of karate, Mr. Khan had slipped on a wet spot on the floor and landed solidly on his back. He complained bitterly of the pain in his lower spine which was radiating down his right leg and was whining about workmen's compensation. Elise performed a physical examination and convinced herself that there was no obvious neurological damage. She reassured Mr. Khan and walked out of the room and over to Nancy.

"Please give Mister Khan, hmmm, let me check the dosage for a ninety-three kilogram Klingon," she said absent mindedly, "One hundred milligrams of Demerol and fifty mg of Vistaril intramuscularly and can we please get x-rays of his back?"

Nancy accepted the orders and Elise said mischievously, "He's pretty wimpy for a warrior, don't you think?" She smiled and winked at the nurse. Then Elise walked over to pick up the next chart and laughed as a short, flamboyantly dressed Ferengi passed her in the hall on the way to visit with his ailing actor friend.

The telemetry radio alarmed. Elise hesitated and then replaced the new chart with the non-urgent complaint back in the rack and walked over to eavesdrop.

"...Thirty-five year old male without past medical history who had acute onset of severe, crushing chest pain while playing racquetball. Vital signs are as follows:..." the paramedic paused as his partner relayed the measurements. "Heart rate - One forty with occasional irregularity, respirations - thirty-two and slightly labored, and blood pressure - One-oh-four over fifty-four." He continued,

"His skin is cool, mottled, and clammy, his lungs are clear. We have an intravenous line established of normal saline running at a moderate rate and have started oxygen by non-rebreather mask. The monitor reads sinus tachycardia with occasional P.V.C.s and short runs of V. tach."

Elise thought that premature ventricular beats and ventricular tachycardia were a very bad sign in a young, supposedly healthy individual. There was a second pause and Elise surmised that Vic, the senior paramedic, was creating some distance between the patient and the radio to finish his report.

"It looks like he's having the big one," he quietly said. "Can I administer morphine?"

The nurse answering the telemetry radio looked questioningly at Elise.

"No, have him give nitro first, cautiously, then morphine. Have them watch his pressure because the nitroglycerin can drop it and it's already low. Have him load the guy with lidocaine for the V. tach and to get their butts in here A.S.A.P.!"


Elise turned and instructed Monica, the charge nurse, to prepare Room Two or Three for a bad cardiac case. She told Wanda to get the patient care technician ready to do an E.K.G. right away. She called over the student, Stacey, and gave her a rundown on the case.

As the paramedics whipped the cart down the corridor, Elise could see that their assessment was entirely accurate. The patient's color was ashen gray and he had a look of abject panic on his face. '*A feeling of impending doom*' was how it was described in the textbooks.

"Doc, I feel like I'm going to die," the husky young man panted.

*Shit*, Elise thought. *There is nothing more ominous than a patient telling you he feels like he is going to die. They are, more often than not, right.*

She took his hand. "Mister..."

"Lansing," supplied Vic.

"Lansing, you may be having a heart attack. We are going to do everything we can to help you. Try to relax." Elise barked out orders to the nurses as the paramedics transferred Mr. Lansing to the hospital gurney and stepped aside.

"God, the pain is intense," the critically ill patient moaned.

Bloods were drawn and monitor leads were placed and hooked up. Elise noted the rhythm had changed to ventricular tachycardia, a regular rhythm emanating from an abnormal area of the heart. She immediately asked for a blood pressure and Monica pressed the button on the monitor to start the blood pressure cuff cycling. The resident ordered a repeat bolus of lidocaine and explained to Mr. Lansing that they would need to shock his heart to convert him back to a normal rhythm.

Suddenly his eyes bulged open wide and then he went totally limp. The monitor sounded as the rhythm deteriorated to ventricular fibrillation, a chaotic wriggling of the heart muscle completely ineffective for pumping blood.

"Charge it up to shock him at two hundred joules!" Elise instructed as she leaned over and pounded Mr. Lansing's chest with her fist, hoping to convert him back into a normal rhythm. It didn't do anything.

The paddles were charged up and, at the beep indicating the machine had achieved maximal intensity, Stacey said, "Ready to shock, everyone clear," as though she were politely inquiring whether her spinster aunt wanted one lump or two of sugar in her tea.

Elise barked, "Clear!"

After making certain she was not touching the patient or the cart, the eager student applied equal firm pressure and discharged the electricity across Mr. Lansing's chest. His body jerked and all eyes turned to the monitor.

"No change, do it again at three hundred joules. And say 'clear' like you mean it. You want people to back off for real," Elise commanded.

The procedure was repeated and this time it worked. Elise gave a sigh of relief when she saw the rhythm on the monitor had converted to a sinus tachycardia, a fast but normally generated rhythm.

Mr. Lansing regained consciousness and said, "Wow, I feel much better, Doc. Can I take that machine home with me when I go?"

The personnel in the room laughed nervously.

"Ah, Mister Lansing, I think it is safe to say that you are going to need to stay in the hospital for a few days. I need to see your E.K.G. to be sure, but I believe you will need medicine which lay people call, 'the clotbuster'. Have you ever had..."

Elise went on to rattle off multiple conditions which would preclude the use of a thrombolytic agent. When Mr. Lansing denied them all, Elise explained to him that he would receive intravenous medication which would hopefully break up any blood clot which might be blocking a coronary artery causing his heart attack.

After the E.K.G. confirmed her suspicions of an acute anterior wall myocardial infarction, Elise instructed his primary nurse to follow the drug protocol precisely and to call her immediately if there were any complications. These agents were very strong and could cause bleeding or other problems. Arrangements to talk to Mr. Lansing's family and to admit him to the intensive care unit were made. The cardiology fellow came down to the E.D. to write the admitting orders. He was apologetic that he had been delayed upstairs taking care of a unit patient in cardiogenic shock. He told Elise that Mr. Lansing was destined to have his coronary arteries studied by angiogram, and probably sooner, rather than later.

Elise walked back to the lounge and filled her mug with coffee. She sat down for a moment, allowing the adrenaline rush to subside. She propped her aching feet on the edge of the couch and let her mind wander.

She started off thinking about the concept of being thirty-five and having a heart attack. This led to the morbid idea of dying prematurely which made her think about Dr. Romano's wife who had committed suicide.

*Linda Morris was a radiologist here and a computer maven*, she recalled. *I bet she had the expertise to alter the C.T. scan. Could Eric have given his grandfather that Antiemezine that morning to simulate stroke symptoms and then colluded with Dr. Morris to create the impression of a bleed on the C.T.? But what actually killed him then? And why would they have done it? Was there really more going on between them and they needed to get disapproving PopPop out of the picture? When did Eric's plane really get in? Why did Linda Morris really kill herself? I just can't believe it's possible.*

*I don't want to believe it*, she thought emphatically.

Her impromptu break over, Elise walked over to the view box and clipped the lumbosacral films up. It was remarkable how much a Klingon's spine resembled a human's! No fracture or other abnormality was present. Elise pulled out a workmen's compensation discharge form and drew the curtain back in Room Eight.

"Mister Khan," she said with a twinkle in her eyes, "Can I write your discharge instructions in English, or would you prefer them in Klingon?"

The painkiller had taken effect and Mr. Khan and his fellow alien found this uproariously funny. He agreed to follow up with the industrial medicine clinic and was oblivious to the stares of the other patients as he was wheeled out to the exit ramp.

As usual, the board was pretty full by this time. Elise took the next chart of an AIDS patient with a fever and headache. She mentally reviewed the gazillion conditions which could cause these nonspecific symptoms as she walked to Room Five.

"Mister Culligan, what seems to be the problem?" Elise started her interview.

Forrest Culligan was a thin forty-two year old white man who looked somewhat disheveled at the moment. He was accompanied by two men approximately his age.

"Cully is my lover, doctor," offered the gentleman standing on the right side of the bed. "I'm Sandy and this is Drew, our friend."

Mr. Culligan apparently didn't feel much like talking so Sandy continued.

"We're both H.I.V.-positive. I am responding well to the protease inhibitors, but Cully was having a hard time meeting the schedule of taking the medicine. His doctor, Doctor Averie, thinks he may be resistant now, because his viral load is up and his CD4 is down. Yesterday he started complaining of a splitting headache. I gave him some Tylenol and didn't think much of it until he started running a fever today."

It was good that Dr. Averie was Mr. Culligan's physician because she was the best infectious disease person in town. She always knew her patients inside out and backwards, and was nice to boot. The residents called her Mother Teresa behind her back because she was so kind and was involved in an organization called Medicine for the Masses. Its goal was to ensure that people all over the world receive quality health care regardless of race, religion, or ability to pay. Every fall, Dr. Averie took off three weeks and traveled to an under-served third world country with this group. Elise was grateful the humanitarian doctor would not be out of reach today for Mr. Culligan.

"Can you talk, Mister Culligan?" Elise asked.

"Call me Cully," he said in response. In her usual observant fashion, Elise noticed he made no eye contact because he was shielding his eyes from the overhead fluorescent light.

"Does the light bother your eyes?"

"Yes," he agreed.

"Do you feel nauseated? Does your neck hurt?" she inquired as she made notations in the chart.

Cully had just about every classical symptom and sign of meningitis including neck stiffness. He was going to require some special tests because, as an AIDS patient, he was liable to have unusual organisms causing his infection. He needed a C.T. scan of his brain to be sure he didn't have an abscess before Elise did his lumbar puncture. Elise wanted to get antibiotics on board quickly. AIDS patients could get run-of-the-mill serious infections in addition to the exotic ones to which they were prone. Fortunately Sean, Mr. Culligan's nurse, understood the urgency and was able to expedite the C.T. scan so Elise could do the spinal tap quickly. She really wanted the cultures to grow out the germ causing his illness. Elise called Dr. Averie and arranged for Mr. Culligan's admission.

"I wish all the doctors were as nice as she is. When I call her, she doesn't ask me a dozen stupid questions or whine about why I'm admitting this patient. She just gives me advice and thanks me for the admission," Elise said to Kristen McCullough, her attending, as she hung up the phone.

The rest of her shift went well and Elise found her thoughts returning to the puzzle of Jefferey Weber on her drive home. She pictured Eric's chiseled features and his laughing blue eyes. She remembered his warm embrace and how safe she felt with him. *No, I just don't believe it at all*, she reaffirmed.

# CHAPTER 14

*Peep, peep, peep, peep.*

Elise wiped and flushed and marveled at the inevitability of being paged whenever it was least convenient to answer it. She washed her hands thoroughly and exited the unisex staff bathroom. The number on her beeper indicated that the call was on an outside line. She sought out the nearest unoccupied phone extension and straddled the chair backwards in a distinctly unladylike fashion.

"Hello, this is Doctor Silver. May I help you?" she asked politely.

"Hi, there. It's me. Did I catch you in the middle of someone?" Eric jested.

"I wish. I just lost someone," Elise told him as she wearily rubbed her eyes. "He was at the athletic club playing tennis and dropped dead of a heart attack. He was seventy-six and in great shape. I have to call his family after I hang up with you. I had just called the code and was in the bathroom when you paged. Actually, it's been a pretty busy day. What's going on there? Is the quality of your drugs up to par today, or should we order from Wyeth?"

Eric laughed a deep belly laugh. Then he took on a tone of feigned indignation, "Do you mean to suggest you would leave me for the competition?"

"You don't have any competition, Eric. I'm yours and yours alone," the resident said in an uncharacteristically serious tone.

On the other end of the phone, Eric cleared his throat. "I'd tell you what I was really thinking, too, except I have a very nosy secretary who is lingering around my desk pretending she has some very important document for me to sign."

His voice muffled, "Barbara, could you go get me some coffee, please? From Starbucks. The one on Diversey, across town! Thanks."

"Excuse me, Elise, but did you want to talk to the floor resident about Bed Four before transport takes her upstairs?" Michelle, the efficient clerk with remarkably bad timing, asked.

"Yes, could you page him for me, please?" Elise responded, dejected that the moment with Eric had passed.

"I'm sorry, I know you are busy. The reason I paged you was my lawyer called. Everything is taken care of. I can make PopPop's donation to the hospital anytime. I was going to call Sid's secretary to set up an appointment. I wanted to know if you wanted to join me."

"I wouldn't miss it for the world!" Elise responded, with a lot more enthusiasm this time. "When did you want to do it?"

"It doesn't matter to me. What does your schedule look like?" he inquired.

"The day after tomorrow would be great. I'm free anytime after morning conference. That ends at ten."

"I'll call and set it up. Could we spend some time together afterwards? I miss you," Eric confessed.

Elise sighed. "I'm sorry my schedule has been so hairy lately. That's what happens when one person is on vacation, another is on maternity leave, the holidays roll around, and I'm the one responsible for making the schedule work. Call me at home tonight after nine and we'll talk. I'm going out with Shelly. Look, I've got to go."

"Elise," Eric started hesitantly.

"Yes?" she answered.

"I really miss you," he said in a husky voice.

"Now *I'm* surrounded by nosy-bodies! Me, too," she compromised.

Now distracted, Elise gave the medicine resident report on Mrs. Compton in Room Four. When she hung up, she found Mr. Kravitz' home phone number. The next of kin was listed as Lila Kravitz, wife. Elise dialed the number and waited as it rang.

"Hello?" an elderly woman answered in a soft quivering voice.

"Mrs. Kravitz?" Elise said.

"Yes, who is this?" she answered.

"This is Doctor Silver from Chicago General Hospital. I work in the emergency department. Your husband was brought here..."

"Oh dear, did Sammy have an accident?" Mrs. Kravitz asked frantically.

"No, it looks like he may have had a heart attack. Do you have any family in town who could come down here with you?" Elise gently suggested.

"Yes, I'll call my son at work. Is Sammy going to be alright?" Mrs. Kravitz asked.

"We will do everything we can for him," Elise assured her. She hated not being entirely truthful, but it was more important to make sure the family members were able to arrive safely. She knew of more than one story of family members having fatal accidents en route to the hospital, and certainly didn't want to be responsible for another.

"We'll be there as soon as we can," the wife asserted.


As she hung up the phone, she noted the second year resident, Frank Lee, waiting patiently at her side. He asked her if he could present a case.

"Sure, I'm free for another one. What have you got?" she encouraged.

"I have a seventy-four year old African American man who has been unable to urinate for twelve hours. He said his urination has been getting slower lately with some dribbling afterward. He hasn't had any fever or chills, and it didn't hurt to urinate earlier today. He denies any previous similar episodes. On physical exam, his abdomen is distended and he is tender in the suprapubic region. His prostate is large with a possible nodule," the resident concluded.

Elise grimaced. "Probably prostate cancer, huh? Well, drop a Foley..."

"I already tried that. We couldn't pass the catheter. Or a coudé for that matter. They are getting hung up in the prostate," Frank replied.

"Did you page urology? I think Paul Starling is on today," Elise suggested.

"Yeah, he's doing a bladder tumor resection, or something. No one else will be available for an hour or so. This guy is pretty uncomfortable," Frank finished.

"OK, let's see what we can do. Who's the nurse?" Elise looked at the chart to see who had signed up to be the nurse. "Tell Didi to get the filiforms and followers set and grab me six-and-a-half gloves, and get yourself a pair. I'll meet you in the room in five minutes."

After checking a few labs and making a few calls, Elise stepped into Room Seven. Derrell Johnson was lying in bed, moaning.

"Oh, Lawdy, please hep me," he entreated.

"Mister Johnson, I'm Doctor Silver. Doctor Lee has explained your problem, and we are going to put a tube in your bladder to drain the pee. You will feel much better soon," she promised.

Elise ran her hands over Mr. Johnson's abdomen as Frank opened the tray containing the instruments.

"Hey, doc, you think it's a boy or a girl?" asked Mr. Johnson's companion, laughing.

"Shut yo face, fool," Mr. Johnson snapped.

Elise fought back a smile by biting the inside of her cheek. Mr. Johnson did, indeed, look about eight months pregnant. His swollen bladder was tense and slightly tender.

"OK, quit torturing him. Why don't you step into the waiting room and we'll come get you when we're done?" Elise instructed.

The thin elderly gentleman rose from his chair. "Can I leave his stuff here?"

"Sure, it'll be safe with us!" Elise answered.

"Probebly safer than wif him!" Mr. Johnson retorted.

After the friend had exited through the curtain, Elise pulled back the cover sheet. She donned a pair of sterile gloves and draped Mr. Johnson's penis with sterile towels. Elise gently retracted the foreskin. Frank liberally applied Betadine to cleanse the urethral opening thoroughly. They injected jelly with anesthetic into the hole. Elise picked up a long thin flexible plastic tube with a flare at one end. Inside that end, there were metal threads visible.

"We gently insert the filiform in until we meet resistance," she said as she demonstrated. The tapered end was inserted in the penis and when the senior resident could not get it in any further, she stopped.

"How are you two doing in there?" Dr. Trumbull asked as he peeked in the curtain. He was abiding by the letter of the regulation that says the attending physician needs to be present for the key portion of the procedure in order to bill for the procedure. Of course, when Elise was the resident doing the procedure, she required minimal supervision.

"We're fine. Mister Johnson, are you doing okay?" Elise said.

"Yep, you gonna be done soon?" he asked.

"Pretty soon," Elise reassured him.

She picked up another filiform and repeated the procedure.

"Alright, you try it now," she encouraged Frank.

He gingerly inserted the filiform and stopped when it would no longer advance.

"Okay, Elise, if you need me, give a holler," Dr. Trumbull offered.

"Thanks, Tom, we will," the senior resident agreed. The attending left the room and drew the curtain shut behind him.

"What's the object here?" Frank asked.

"You keep doing this 'til one actually finds the narrowed passage into the bladder," she explained as she continued to insert filiforms. Mr. Johnson's penis had four of the tubes sticking out before Elise made a satisfied grunt.

"There, that one is in," she remarked as this filiform was able to advance all the way. "Quick, grab the container."

Frank scrambled to get the plastic container in position as dark yellow urine came gushing out the end of the filiform. The residents removed the filiforms which had met dead ends and were unable to advance into the bladder.

"Now we screw the followers in one at a time, the smallest one first," Elise said as she picked up the first one.

It was another tube which screwed into those threads in the exposed end of the successful filiform. The follower was then pushed in the urethra, causing the filiform to curl up in the bladder.

They then withdrew the apparatus out enough so they could access the threaded end of the filiform. After unscrewing the follower in use, they chose the next larger sized follower and then connected it to the filiform. Elise allowed Frank to continue the procedure once he understood the process. They inserted progressively larger followers which dilated the entrance to the bladder. Finally the doctors were able to place a rubber catheter into the bladder to remain there to allow the urine to drain into a bag.

"If we had been unsuccessful, we would have had to place a suprapubic catheter in to empty his bladder. Have you ever seen one of those?"

Frank shook his head in the negative.

"You make a small incision above the pubic bone and put the Foley in through the abdominal wall. Review it in the procedure book. In the meantime, we'll have the nurse instruct him on how to care for the leg bag, and leave it in until he can see the urologist. Make sure you send off a urinalysis and a culture and put him on antibiotics prophylactically," Elise said.

"This thing is going to stay in me? I feel like I have to use it," Mr. Johnson complained.

"That feeling will go away, Mister Johnson. Your pee is collecting in this bag. We suspect you have a large prostate and you may need surgery to fix it. You will need to talk to the specialists to decide what has to be done," Elise said as she opted not to mention the possibility of cancer. Better for the urologists to confirm it than for her to worry the patient needlessly.

Mr. Johnson felt quite relieved now that his bladder was emptied. He understood his follow-up instructions and promised to take his medicine and make an appointment with the specialist. Elise left him in the room to await the nurse for his final written directions. Elise told Frank to let Dr. Trumbull know that he should go chat with Mr. Johnson before he was discharged.

Elise walked to the chart rack and removed the clipboard on Bed Ten. Jaylen Dixon was a three-year-old black child whose mother had brought him in because, '*he wasn't acting right.*' The resident flipped through the lab results and wrinkled her brow.

"Tom, can I talk to you for a minute," she asked her attending, somewhat aggravated that the answer was escaping her. The usually confident resident had just recently become comfortable with Dr. Trumbull. He was a brilliant physician with a very intense personality. He had recently satiated his intermittent wanderlust by spending several months in Africa exploring his roots and tending to ailing Ethiopians. Elise was rarely intimidated, but Tom Trumbull was a rare individual.

"Sure. Elise, what's up?" he replied.

"I have a three year old black boy whose mom brought him in for abnormal behavior. She said he had been complaining of a stomachache and headaches. Since yesterday he's been lethargic and confused. He's been vomiting also. On exam, he looks sick, but his neuro exam is nonfocal. There is no evidence of an acute abdomen. I've done screening labs and a C.T. didn't show anything. I thought of sepsis so I did a septic work-up. The urine was negative and the chest x-ray was clear. His urine drug screen was negative. He had a therapeutic acetaminophen level. The only thing his labs did show was a hemolytic anemia. His sickle cell screen is positive for being a carrier. Even though the mother didn't notice a fever, I was thinking Reye's syndrome. The liver enzymes are slightly elevated, but the bilirubin and alkaline phosphatase are normal. I'm stumped," she concluded her presentation.

"Let's go see him," Dr. Trumbull suggested.

Dr. Trumbull surveyed the small form in the gurney. Jaylen was small for his age, and he was lying still on the bed. He did open his eyes temporarily when Dr. Trumbull said his name loudly. He then went back to sleep. Dr. Trumbull was unable to get him to focus or follow any commands. He blew on his huge dark brown hands and rubbed them together to warm them up before examining the boy's abdomen. Again, there was no evidence of a surgical cause for his abdominal pain. Dr. Trumbull asked the mother some questions.

"How has he been developing?"

The child's mother replied, "He be kinda slow. He don't talk much. He like playin' ball, though, doncha, Boo?" She stroked the boy's nappy hair. He didn't seem to respond.

Dr. Trumbull referred to the chart. The next of kin was listed at *Kasandra Williams.* Their address was a local housing project and their payer status was Medicaid.

"Miss Williams, has he been complaining of any other kinds of pains lately?" Dr. Trumbull inquired.

"His legs are always paining him. I just figgered they were growing pains," his mother offered.

"Miss Williams, what is your apartment like?" the attending asked gently.

"The damn landlord don't do nothing to keep it up. The pipes is rusting and we lucky when the hot water works. I had to fight to get them to put bars up on the windows 'cause there ain't no screens and I was afraid Jayjay would fall out. There's cockroaches everywhere!" she angrily described.

"Uh-huh, I see," Dr. Trumbull responded. "Miss Williams, Doctor Silver and I are going to go look at Jaylen's x-rays and discuss his case. We think he is sick, and we want to help him get better. We'll be back."

After they had left the room and were no longer in earshot, Elise said, "Well, Tom, I have to confess I'm still stumped. You seem to have an idea, though. What are you thinking?"

"I do have an idea," he answered.

Dr. Trumbull pulled the chest x-ray films out of their folder and clipped them onto the viewing screen.

"What do you see?" he asked didactically.

Elise described the film. She did it systematically, the way she had been taught. She described the heart and lungs and ribs.

"No infiltrate, the heart size is normal, no new or healed fractured ribs suggesting abuse," she summarized.

"What do you make of that?" Dr. Trumbull asked as he pointed to some white chips in the stomach.

Elise thought for a moment. Tentatively she guessed, "Pill fragments? But the tox screen was negative."

"How about paint flecks?" Dr. Trumbull offered.

"I'm sorry, Tom, this is still not coming together for me," Elise admitted.

"I'm glad to see I can still teach you a thing or two, Elise. I love to feel like I'm earning my salary." He ticked off the positive findings on his fingers. "One, headache, confusion, slow development, encephalopathy. Two, abdominal pain, vomiting. Three, bone pains. Four, hemolytic anemia and slightly elevated liver enzymes. Finally, radio-opaque paint chips in the stomach in a poorly kept up environment."

It still didn't register with Elise.

Dr. Trumbull ended with, "I think Jaylen has lead poisoning."

"That makes sense. Wow, I've never seen it before," she paused. "Maybe I have, but didn't recognize it. I better go look up the treatment and make arrangements for him to be admitted. I'll write the orders for the lead level and talk to Mom, too. Thanks, Tom. Pretty cool case, huh?"

"You did a good work-up, Elise. You just can't diagnose something if you don't think of it," he instructed.

"Elise, the wife and son of Bed Two are here. They're in the Quiet Room. I've already paged Pastoral Care," Michelle informed Elise.

"Thanks, Michey. You're the best," Elise said. She finished making a notation in the chart and then handed it to the secretary.

The resident straightened her hair, buttoned her lab coat, and sighed. This was probably her least favorite thing to do, even worse than packing a bleeding nose or taking an ingrown toenail off. She saw the clergyman enter the department and walked over to him.

"Hello, Father. Thanks for coming down," she greeted him.

"Does he need last rites?" inquired the priest, trying to get up to speed on the patient's condition.

"No, he was Jewish," Elise stated.

They walked silently to the Quiet Room, the area reserved for family members of patients who were critically ill, or worse. Elise opened the door and walked in first, introducing herself and Father Flanagan. Mrs. Kravitz sat on the worn green couch with her middle-aged son seated next to her. He had his arm around his mother protectively.

"How is Dad?" he asked immediately.

"I'm sorry, I have bad news. Mister Kravitz had a heart attack at the health club and we were unable to save him. The paramedics worked hard on him and we tried everything we could, but it was too late. If it is any consolation, I think he went quickly and painlessly."

The elderly woman looked pale and very tired. She shook her head back and forth.

"Donny, it's okay, Dad's okay," she said.

"Ma, the doctor just told us Dad died," her son reiterated in a cracking voice.

"Yes, dear, I heard her. It's just that we got the Palm Beach Post yesterday at that fancy newsstand to see what the snowbirds were doing and Dad was reading it at breakfast. In the obituaries, it said that Jacob Richter, you remember him from when we lived downtown?"

Donny shook his head yes. "The piano player?"

"Yes, that's the one. Anyway, he passed away of a heart attack in the middle of a match at their country club. He was ahead in sets. Dad said to me, 'That wouldn't be a bad way to go, would it?' I think he knew it was his time, somehow." And at that, Mrs. Kravitz put her head in her hands and wept quietly for her husband of fifty years.

A chill went down Elise's spine. It was kind of eerie and coincidental. She let the woman cry for a time and then asked if she would like to see her husband. Mrs. Kravitz composed herself and affirmed that she would.

As Father Flanagan escorted Mrs. Kravitz and Don to the now tidied code room, Elise daydreamed about her own future and mortality. *Do I really know Eric as well as I think I do? Could he have been involved with Linda Morris? Could they have orchestrated Mr. Weber's death? Or did Sid Shulman do it? Why can't I make these pieces fit either?!* she thought frustratedly.

The rest of her shift was a blur. That night she was talking to Shelly at dinner and asked her if she thought someone she was dating could hide a huge secret without her knowing.

"Not having been in the position in quite some time, I can only speculate. No, I pretty much think I'm a good judge of character. But you know every once in a while I'll see a story in the newspaper about some woman who discovers her husband has another wife in another state or he murdered an ex-girlfriend fifteen years before and I just can't understand how she could not tell something was wrong." Shelly laughingly asked, "Why? What do you think Eric has done?"

Elise really didn't want to go into the particulars and rapidly changed the subject. Shelly noticed, but tactfully decided not to push her sister.

When they finished eating, Elise tried to pick up the bill. Her wealthy sister magnanimously took the check from her hand and handed the waitress her credit card.

"I love you dearly, but I can't tolerate watching you use your wallet tip table. It makes me crazy."

"Thanks, Shel. Someday when I'm rich too, I'll return the favor," Elise promised.

# CHAPTER 15

Her mind wandered as Dr. Kostas finished his discussion on fractures of the upper extremity. Elise was far too excited and nervous about confronting Sid Shulman with Eric. In fact, Dr. Kostas had concluded his talk and was waiting for Elise to acknowledge him when her attention shifted back to Friday morning conference.

"Are there any more questions?" she said and paused expectantly. None were forthcoming. "Then I would like to thank Doctor Kostas from the department of orthopedics for an excellent lecture on upper extremity fractures. Your radiographs were super. Thank you for coming. Next week we are going to have oral boards simulations. Conference will start at eight o'clock sharp."

The residents considered themselves dismissed and filtered out of the room quickly. Elise collected her stuff and scooted to the chief resident's office. She filed the extra handouts in the filing cabinet. The slide projector went back in the closet.

There was a tap at the door. Eric was standing there in a wool navy suit with narrow pinstripes. He had on a barely cream-colored shirt and an expensive silk tie with a navy, red, and cream pattern.

"You look really handsome, Eric," Elise remarked.

Eric looked Elise over. She was wearing a royal blue suit the color of the Pacific on a lazy summer day. She had accessorized with dainty gold earrings with blue cubic zirconia and a plain gold chain around her long, lovely neck. Her black pumps accentuated the line of her calves and were the perfect height for her. She brushed back a wisp of her auburn hair and blushed a little under his scrutiny.

"Thank you. You look beautiful yourself," he admired. "Are you ready to go?"

"I sure am. Have you figured out how we are going to see if Doctor Shulman was the one?" Elise asked.

"No, I'm not exactly sure how to do it. I guess I'll give him the check and wing it."

They walked down the hall to the elevators. Elise pressed the up button and they waited.

"Be thankful it isn't three-thirty - we'd have to wait forever for the elevator!" she remarked.

The doors opened and an attractive black woman exited pushing a cart of mail. She smiled in greeting as Elise held the elevator door open with her hand. After she had passed, the couple got on the elevator. Elise pushed the button for the twelfth floor where all the bigwigs had their offices.

After several requisite interim stops, the elevator opened up on the top floor. They glanced at each other, took deep breaths, stepped briskly off the elevator. Turning to the right, they saw the secretary for the president of the hospital.

"Hello, I'm Eric Weber and I have an appointment with Sid," Eric declared.

"He's expecting you. I'll let him know you are here. Can I get either of you a cup of coffee or a pop?" the secretary said in a professional voice.

"No, thank you," Eric declined.

"None for me either, thanks," Elise seconded.

"Would you like to have a seat over there?" she requested.

Eric and Elise walked over to the couch. He picked up the *Newsweek* laying on the coffee table, absently shuffled through the pages, and then replaced it on the table.

Elise looked around. *You would never know the hospital was in trouble looking at the decor up here,* she thought wryly to herself.

"Doctor Shulman is ready for you now," his secretary announced. She was standing in front of them, smiling. As they stood up, she began walking down the hall to show them the way. She knocked on the first door on the left.

"Doctor Shulman, Mister Weber is here," she perfunctorily repeated at the open door.

"Eric, my boy, come on in," Sid said warmly. He offered Eric his right hand and grasped Eric's hand tightly with both of his. "I can't tell you again how sorry I am about Jeff. Chicago General felt his loss profoundly, as did I. I considered him one of my oldest friends. I miss him sorely. How are you doing?"

Elise was struck by how sincere Dr. Shulman sounded. It was hard to remember the reason they were there was to explore the possibility that he had intentionally murdered Eric's grandfather.

"I'm doing as well as can be expected, Sid. I miss PopPop terribly. Oh, I'm sorry, do you know my girlfriend, Doctor Elise Silver?" he introduced her.

"Yes, you look very familiar. The emergency department, is it?" Sid said a trifle hesitantly.

"Yes, Doctor Shulman. I'm impressed," Elise responded.

"I'm pretty good at faces, but not quite so good with names. Elise, nice to see you again," he said and extended his hand out to shake hers as well. "What can I do for you, son?"

He motioned them over to an area of his office which had two cushioned chairs and a loveseat arranged around a table. They sat down, and Sid was considerably more relaxed than the duo.

"Actually, it's what we can do for you. Sid, you know that C.G.H. was very important to my grandparents," Eric said. "PopPop wanted me to make this contribution to the hospital. His will specified that you use the money whatever way you see fit."

Eric held out the check and Sid accepted it graciously. He looked at the amount and his eyebrows rose registering his shock. Elise took the opportunity to call him on it.

"Doctor Shulman, you seem surprised," she noted.

The elderly physician took off his bifocal spectacles and rubbed his bushy gray eyebrows and tired, gray eyes.

"Eric, I'm so sorry. It's all my fault. I feel so guilty," he lamented in a cracking voice.

*Well, that was a lot easier than I thought*, Elise thought. *It never seems to be that easy on T.V. You usually have to wring the confession out in the last three minutes of the hour-long episode right after the last set of inane commercials.*

"What do you mean?" Eric asked, obviously thinking the same thing Elise was.

Sid stood up and walked over to the window overlooking the parking lot. The Hancock building loomed above the angular Chicago skyline and one could even see a pinch of the lake in the far corner. He was silent for a moment. Then he shook his head and began, "Eric, don't you need this money?"

Confused, Eric asked, "Why would I need that money? PopPop wanted to donate it to the hospital."

"Did Jeff ever tell you the whole story about Deegan Stone?" Sid asked Eric.

Eric looked at Sid with a puzzled look on his face. "The financial planner who ran off with PopPop's money?" he clarified.

"Yes, that's the man," Sid confirmed.

Elise and Eric waited befuddled until Sid continued.

"Eric, I was the person who recommended Deegan to your grandfather. We had been working together for almost six years and he had been doing such a good job with my investments that I gave him your grandfather's name. Deegan got involved with some bad deals and then his wife divorced him. I think he went off the deep end. In any case, he ripped us off. Your grandfather, several other clients to whom I had referred Deegan, and I lost a great deal of money. All I had left was my retirement pension from C.G.H. And it was all my fault that your grandfather was taken in. I feel so bad about this."

It was Elise and Eric's turn to be shocked. If Sid knew about PopPop's financial misfortunes, then obviously he wouldn't have bumped him off to fill C.G.H.'s faltering coffers.

"So, I'm asking you, will you be okay if C.G.H. gets this endowment?" Sid finished.

"Sid, I'm very sorry to hear about your trouble. My grandfather didn't leave me a lot of money, but I own my home and I make a good living. Please don't worry about me. I hope the money will help C.G.H. And I hope things turn out all right for you and Emily. I think you should stop feeling guilty about PopPop. Money didn't mean much to him. I know he considered you a close friend," Eric reassured the older neurologist.

"Thank you, son. His friendship meant a lot to me, too," Sid reiterated. His craggy countenance brightened and he looked as though a great weight had been lifted off his shoulders. "Well then, on behalf of Chicago General Hospital, thank you for this most generous check."

Once safely on the elevator and alone, Elise turned to Eric and said, "Well, we're back to square one! He certainly had no motive, since he didn't think your grandfather would be a source of funds for the hospital. Who killed your grandfather and why?!"

"I don't know, Elise. I just don't know," he answered hollowly.

# CHAPTER 16

"So what are you doing for New Year's Eve?" Janice asked Elise.

"I don't have any plans yet. What are you guys doing?" she questioned.

"Don and I are going to a big bash at my advisor's house. You know, the one who won the lottery. Frankly, I'd rather have him give me a hundred thousand dollars than a party invite but I guess beggars can't be choosers," the family practice resident answered.

"Oh yeah, Eric was invited, too. He lives a couple of houses away from Doctor Romano. He hasn't asked me yet." Elise heard a faint beep. "Can you hold on, I'm getting call waiting."

She depressed the *flash* button and greeted her other caller.

"It's me. It occurred to me that we talked about that party, but I didn't actually invite you. Would you be my guest and spend New Year's Eve with me?" Eric asked.

"I'm on the other line. Could I call you back?" Elise responded coolly.

"Sure," he replied.

She clicked back to Janice. "It was him. He invited me to the party- impressive timing, huh?"

"Great! We can go together."

"I'm not sure if I want to go," Elise said dubiously.

Janice was aware that something was going on between Eric and Elise, but she did not know the circumstances. She also knew Elise well enough to know the details would be forthcoming when she was ready. Janice hoped that they'd work whatever it was out, because she had never seen Elise so happy with someone before.

Elise changed the subject, "I got the most amazing call the other day. The director of the E.D. at the Cleveland Clinic called trying to recruit me. He said someone had highly recommended me. I guess they are expanding rapidly and a neighboring hospital had to shut down. He needs to increase their staffing. The set-up sounds pretty sweet. He invited me to come check them out."

"Pretty impressive. It must be nice to be in a specialty where they seek you out, rather than having to find your own job," Janice compared.

"No, actually I found this kind of odd. I guess if I go for the interview, I should find out who it was who suggested he contact me," Elise replied.

"Well, I hope you change your mind about going to the New Year's Eve party. See you for lunch on Friday?"

"Same Bat-time, same Bat-channel. TTFN. Ta ta for now," Elise replied in her best Tigger-voice.


Elise steeled herself and dialed Eric's number. They chatted for a while and Eric had the distinct impression that there was something very wrong. When he pressed her to discover what it was, he hit a brick wall.

"I think we need to talk," Eric observed.

Elise sighed. "I think you're right. Do you want to come over?"

Eric said he'd be right over and Elise replaced the handset. She ran through her mind what she wanted to say. She just knew she had to be wrong.

When he arrived, he leaned down to kiss Elise. She tensed slightly and drew away. Eric was totally perplexed.

"I'm really sorry I didn't invite you sooner. I guess I just assumed that it was a done deal and we would be spending New Year's Eve together. I shouldn't have made a unilateral decision like that and I apologize."

Elise winced. He was such a nice guy and she didn't want to lose him. Or he was a slick sociopath who probably would kill her right here, hack her up into tiny manageable pieces, and attempt to discard the remains in the garbage disposal when she confronted him with her suspicions. She figured she'd lose either way. The resident had run through multiple scenarios and ways to address this confrontation, and had been unable to find one which was palatable to her. She decided she needed to just get it out and see what happened.

"Eric, did you give your grandfather Antiemezine?" she asked.

"What are you talking about?" he said incredulously.

"I saw the pills. You're not going to deny that you have Antiemezine in your grandfather's medicine cabinet, are you? From your laboratory. Hidden behind the Pepto-Bismol," she accused him.

Eric furrowed his brow and thought. A look of recognition flashed across his face.

"Oh, that. Remember on our first date I was getting over the stomach flu? Well, the Antiemezine was for the puking and the Pepto-Bismol was for the diarrhea," he explained.

"Then why was it in your grandfather's cabinet?" she fired back.

"Because I was too sick to go up and down the stairs. I crashed on the couch for twenty-four hours, drinking apple juice and chamomile tea. What the hell is going on with you?" he asked in indignation.

Elise threw her arms around his neck and tried to kiss him. She just knew it had to be the truth! They might never bring the real culprit to justice, but she was certain Eric was not his grandfather's murderer.

Coldly he pried her hands away and stood waiting for an explanation.

"After we ruled out Doctor Shulman as the murderer, my imagination started running rampant on me. I started thinking maybe there was more about your relationship with Linda than you were telling me. Maybe you cared enough about her to eliminate your grandfather from the picture. Deep down I knew it was stupid, but there was Antiemezine in your medicine cabinet and insecurity in my heart! I'm so sorry, Eric!"

Elise spent half the night convincing Eric that she really did trust him, pleading until he finally forgave her. She then spent the rest of the night showing him just how much she had grown to care for him.

In the morning, they were still cuddling in a semi-sleep when the telephone rang. Elise lazily rolled over and picked up the receiver. Suddenly, she bolted upright, wide awake.

"So what did you find out?" she asked excitedly as she switched over to speakerphone.

Mark answered," Well, there was only one thing in his system other than his daily medications."

"It wasn't Antiemezine, was it," Elise stated matter-of-factly as she smiled confidently at Eric.

"Nope."

"Well, don't keep us in suspense!" she implored.

"Us?" Mark questioned and Elise could envision his eyebrows raising.

"Mark!" she snapped.

"Ok, ok. It was haloperidol," he revealed.

Elise shot her arms straight above her head to signal a touchdown.

"Yes! I owe you my firstborn for this, Mark," Elise thanked him.

"Cool! Can I expect it you to deliver it nine months from now?" he double-entendred mischievously.

"Pig!" she teased back.

"That's me."

"Seriously, you're a prince! Thanks, Mark, I really do owe you one."

"Anytime," he concluded and they hung up.

"So what exactly does that mean?" Eric looked for clarification.

Elise explained that haloperidol was a potent drug used on psychiatric patients which could cause a dystonic reaction as an undesirable side effect.

"But how did PopPop get it in his system? He didn't have any psychiatric problem. I'm sure he didn't take that medicine," Eric wondered.

"That, my dear Watson, is the sixty-four thousand dollar question," Elise replied.

They tabled the discussion long enough to take a luxurious, steaming hot shower. Eric called his secretary to tell her he wouldn't be in until later. They walked hand in hand into the kitchen-dining area.

As Eric read the Tribune aloud, Elise conjured up a mushroom-cheese omelet and some whole-wheat toast. She poured Eric a mug of steaming decaf hazelnut coffee and he sighed.

"This is the time I miss my grandfather the most," he shared.

Elise served him his breakfast, sat down beside him and cradled her mug.

"Really, why?" she asked as she deeply inhaled the rich coffee aroma.

"We had our morning ritual. I would give PopPop his pills for the day and he would cook breakfast while I read him the newspaper. He especially liked Ann Landers and the editorial page, and, of course, the lottery numbers every Sunday and Thursday morning," he reminisced as he ate his eggs.

"Would he take his medications himself if you weren't around?"

"Heck, no. His eyesight was abominable because of his cataracts. I would either lay out several days' in a row or Doc Tony would come over and do it. A lot of times Doc Tony would join PopPop for breakfast. Linda usually had to be at the hospital earlier than he did. In fact, I was having breakfast with him just the other day and we were talking about those days. We even talked about you," Eric confessed shyly.

A light bulb went off in Elise's head. You just can't diagnose something if you don't think of it.

"So Doctor Romano would dole out your grandfather's pills if you couldn't?"

"Yes," he reaffirmed.

"Eric, didn't you have a business trip just before your grandfather died?" Elise explored.

"Yes. I left Saturday evening to get the cheaper airfare and returned the morning he passed away."

"Do you remember if you laid out his meds before you went?" Elise continued to probe.

Eric paused a moment to think. "As a matter of fact, I know I couldn't have because PopPop had to pick up his prescription renewals a few days after I left. Doc Tony must have laid them out for him."

He looked at her and said discouragingly, "There's no way Doc Tony could have harmed my grandfather. They were friends for years."

"Mmhmm," Elise mumbled. *I've seen people shot for drinking the last beer in the fridge and stabbed in the head by a sister for not taking her socks off,* she wryly thought. *I believe anything is possible.*

She abruptly changed the subject. "I wish I didn't have to go to work today," she pouted.

"You have tomorrow off, don't you?"

"Actually, I have the next four days off except for Friday morning conference! It's nice to be the one making the schedule at holiday time. Of course, I worked Christmas Eve and Day like I do every year."

"So you haven't answered me yet. Will you spend New Year's Eve with me? We don't have to go to Doc Tony's party if you don't want to," he offered as a compromise.

"Oh no," Elise responded. "I wouldn't miss that for the world! Besides Janice is invited too. Maybe I'll go buy a new dress tomorrow."

They cleared the table and placed the dishes in the dishwasher. Eric gave Elise a kiss and bid her farewell to go home to get changed for work. Elise dressed and left the apartment herself, off to provide some relief to the afternoon crew at Chicago General Emergency Department.

# CHAPTER 17

As was often the case, the department was up for grabs when Elise arrived for her one to eleven swing shift. Her attending, Dr. Patel, greeted her appreciatively and promptly relinquished the intern to her care.

Jack Jamison, M.D. stood patiently waiting until Elise indicated she was ready for his presentation and then he began.

"I'm not sure what to do with this case..."

Elise thought wearily, *that's why you're the intern and I'm the third year resident.* She smiled encouragingly and Jack relaxed and continued.

"Mister Fong is an ninety-two year old Chinese gentleman who speaks minimal English and has been less responsive since yesterday. He is febrile, but I have yet to locate the source of his fever," he said.

"So far sounds pretty straightforward - sepsis work-up." Elise decided to be specific so Jack would order all the tests which she felt were appropriate. "Check his blood and urine for evidence of infection and do a chest x-ray, too."

"That's not the part that I'm concerned about," he said, a bit miffed that she felt it necessary to review such a basic work-up with him almost halfway through the year. He explained, "Mister Fong has bruises all over his chest and back. I've never handled elder abuse and don't know what the proper procedure to report it is."

Elise raised her eyebrows skeptically and asked, "Did you mention your findings to the family?"

"Oh no," he answered. "I didn't want to alert them that I was suspicious."

"Let's go see him together," the more experienced doctor suggested and led the way to Room Six.

They walked in to find a frail, ill-appearing Oriental man in a semi-upright position, propped up by down pillows from home. The pillowcases were ancient and slightly frayed, but clean. To have pillows in the E.D., the nursing staff either had to steal them from another floor or you had to bring your own from home. Elise was determined to bequeath a dozen pillows, earmarked to be irreversibly chained to the gurneys, to the department when she passed beyond the shadowy veil. Mr. Fong's eyes were shut and his breathing was rapid and shallow. His face had wrinkles on its wrinkles resembling a Shar-Pei and Elise doubted he was actually only ninety-two years old as his chart suggested. He looked closer to two hundred.

Elise explained that she was supervising Dr. Jamison and asked that the granddaughter tell Mr. Fong that she needed to examine him as well.

"*Tong?*" Elise asked as she demonstrated her entire command of the Cantonese Chinese dialect. Mr. Fong shook his head to deny any pain but his eyelids remained closed.

Elise appraised his chest. Mr. Fong's ribs jutted out and his translucent skin was hot to the touch. There were multiple circular bruises approximately two and a half inches in diameter randomly distributed over the back and chest, purplish and blotchy in some areas, yellow-green in others. The overlying skin was intact without abrasion and the resident noted that the lesions were not raised as she ran her fingers nimbly over them. His lungs sounded quite junky when Elise listened through her stethoscope.

"How did he get these bruises?" Elise directly confronted Mr. Fong's granddaughter.

Her English was broken, but intelligible. "Ancient Chinese cure. Take glass and make hot. Put to skin."

"I thought the Chinese venerated their elders!" Jack could no longer contain his ire.

"Relax, Jack," Elise soothed. "Ma'am, *why* do you do this?" Elise entreated the woman to explain.

"Draw out bad spirits. Make *Ai-yeh* well."

"I understand. We would like to do tests to try to find out why your grandfather is so sick, but he will need to stay in the hospital for treatment. Who is his doctor?"

"Doctor Chan has office in Chinatown. Sees *Ai-yeh* there," the middle-aged Chinese woman replied.

In the hallway, Elise further explained to Jack that cupping was common in the elderly Chinese population as were many other folk remedies. She gave him an impromptu dissertation on other cultures' medical customs and beliefs.

"We may not agree with their ways, but we must respect them," Elise finished. "However, I do appreciate how concerned you were for the patient's safety. Keep up the vigilance, and you may save someone's life someday."


"Elise, Doctor Pinchon is in Room Twelve," Leslee, the charge nurse for the day, informed her as she held out the V.I.P.'s chart.

"Thanks," Elise said as she accepted it and wheeled around to go to the Cast Room.

"Doctor Pinchon, again?! What were you doing *this* time?" Elise gently teased the elderly physician. Dr. Pinchon had been a very valuable part of the medical staff in his heyday and was enjoying retirement, maybe too much. His right shoulder had the propensity for dislocating with minimal provocation, and from the looks of the angle of his arm, he had done it again.

Dr. Pinchon lowered the front section of the Tribune, awkwardly as he only had use of his left hand. He responded sheepishly, "I was diving into the pool at the club and *POP*! Out she came. I tried to fix it myself, but I decided you were so pretty to look at, I'd come visit you instead."

Elise laughed. "If I didn't know better, I'd think you like Versed and morphine. I'm going to check that out today. We're going to use something different."

Something was nagging at the back of Elise's subconscious. She asked, "May I see your paper, please?"

"Sure, young lady," he agreed as he offered her the folded paper.

Preoccupied, she corrected him as she scanned the front page, "That's Doctor Young Lady to you!"

In the top left corner of the paper, there was something about the state lottery in smallish type. There had been no winner and the grand prize was now up to sixteen million dollars. The headline referred the reader to an inside page for the actual numbers. An idea began to germinate in Elise's brain.

"Well, Doctor Pinchon, you know the routine. First we x-ray you, then we give you the good drugs and reduce the dislocation, then back to Xrayland."

"Elise, dear, can we forego the pre-reduction films? I'll take my chances that there is no fracture. I have a meeting of the Masons tonight and don't want to drag this out."

"Of course. I'll send the nurse in right away and we'll get started," Elise promised.

"Could you ask the pretty one with the glasses to come in and help? She holds my hand. If you do, I'll let you teach one of your underlings on me," he cajoled.

"Great!"

Elise walked to the nurses' station and waited for Jack to be free. She then instructed him to go to the reference books and review the technique for reducing the shoulder joint back into place. As she did, she saw out of the corner of her eye, Dr. Romano leaving Room Seven.

"Ann, do you have the Cast Room?" she called out.

"No, but do you need help? I just love the old geezer, except when he pats my butt," Ann replied cheerfully.

"Let's grab some Brevital," Elise suggested.

She followed Ann to the locked medication cabinet. "Does Doctor Romano stop in the E.D. often?" she asked innocently.

Few family doctors entered the realm of the emergency department, even if their personal patients were brought in. The emergency physicians would manage the patients while they were in the E.D. Then the private physician would be contacted, but would either follow the patient up in the office in the days following, or would see the patient on the floor after admission.

"Actually, he is one of the few docs who does. Doc Tony used to bypass the E.D. all the time, but the insurance companies have put the kibosh on direct admissions. He has a great rapport with his patients and they love him, so, if he's in the house when his patient is here, he tries to stop on down," the blonde nurse answered as she signed for the narcotic.

The two women grabbed Jack on their way back to Room Twelve. Elise positioned herself towards the head of the bed on his left side and wrapped a sheet around Dr. Pinchon, in slingshot fashion looping in his right armpit. She would provide the countertraction to keep the patient from being pulled off the gurney when the intern manipulated the arm back into the socket. Jack secured Dr. Pinchon's affected right arm with another sheet and he grimaced.

"Time for the giddy juice, Elise. By the way, where are your glasses, honey?" he asked Ann, trying to keep his mind off the unpleasant task at hand.

Elise ordered the medications and Ann slowly administered them as she answered, "I had Lasik. Don't you like this better?"

"Oh yes, I can see yir beeyutifool eyez. Don't fergitto hold mmwhamimrrorf," he slurred and his eyelids drooped as the drugs hit him like a Mack truck.

"I think he's ready, " Elise giggled. "Ann, I'll translate. First he sexually harassed you by making a totally inappropriate comment about your eyes, and then he compounded it by asking you to hold his, I sure hope it was, hand."

The respiratory therapist lightly touched Dr. Pinchon's eyelashes and noted the absence of a blink response. She repositioned his pulse oximeter probe and then motioned to Elise. The determined resident shifted her weight back, dug her heels into the ground and nodded to Jack , saying, "Whenever you are ready."

Jack began pulling on the arm and Elise gently redirected his traction more downward than out. After he shifted, he leaned all his weight back. His biceps bulged and beads of sweat popped out on his brow. Suddenly, there was a perceptible movement of the joint and then a loud click as the arm bone slipped back into the shoulder joint.

"It's all in the relaxation, Jack. If you are too stingy with the drugs, you can have a devilish time putting the joint back in," Elise shared her experience with the intern.

The medical entourage removed the sheets to the joyous accompaniment of Dr. Pinchon's snoring. Elise instructed Ann to watch his oxygen saturation and make sure he was getting enough oxygen now that the pain stimulus had been removed and the medications' effects were unopposed. Ann slipped the post-reduction x-ray requisition out of the chart and wheeled Dr. Pinchon over to Radiology herself.

"Be back in a sec," she announced as she left the department.

Elise walked over to the chart rack to see what cases were waiting to be brought in, commenting on how unusual it was to be so busy right before the holiday. She scanned down the slots and one towards the bottom caught her eye. She read it, then removed it and checked the triage nurse signature incredulously. She frowned when she realized it was Phyllis Fields, R.N., a neophyte in the emergency department.

"Leslee," she called. "You'd better get this one in pronto and in a Gyne room. It's a twenty-four year old woman whose last period was November twelfth who had acute onset of abdominal pain two hours prior to triage and is now dizzy. She's already waited forty-five minutes."

Leslee's eyes widened and they exchanged knowing glances. Within minutes, Ms. Curtis was ensconced in Room Ten surrounded by personnel. She looked even worse than the triage note would have led Elise to believe. Her skin was cool and clammy and she was slightly confused. She needed to be helped onto the cart and the nurses had to undress her. They repeated her vital signs and found her blood pressure to be very low.

Elise fired orders, "I want two large bore I.V.s and run the fluids in wide open. Put a Foley catheter in her to grab a specimen of urine and do a pregnancy test on it right away, please."

Her examination was even more concerning. Ms. Curtis had a very tender lower abdomen and there was a scant amount of blood in her vagina. By the time Elise had finished the pelvic, the nurse who had taken the sample of urine was able to call into the room, informing Elise that the pregnancy test was, indeed, positive.

Elise motioned to Leslee to press the intercom button, and she complied.

"Michelle, two things. Get OB-Gyne down here *STAT* and tell Vakesh and Jack to come into Room Ten right away," she projected from her stool at the foot of the bed.

"Consider it done," answered the efficient clerk.

Elise asked Diana, the nurse assigned to the Gyne room for the shift, to assemble the equipment to perform a culdocentesis. She explained to the patient and Jack as she organized her tools.

"Miss Curtis, I am very concerned that you may have a tubal, or ectopic, pregnancy. This means that the egg has started growing in the wrong place and your body is unable to sustain it. The embryo continues to develop until it gets too big, and then it ruptures the fallopian tube. If this happens, you can die. I need to check to see if there is blood already collecting inside you."

"Okay. How do you do that?" Ms. Curtis asked.

"You are not very sensitive near the opening to your uterus, which comes in handy during childbirth. I will stick a needle in there and see if there is fluid in your pelvis. Do I have your consent to do this?" Elise asked.

Since this was really an emergent procedure, Elise did not really need to consent the patient formally. However, if it could be done quickly and would not slow down the care of the patient, Elise preferred to go by the book.

"Yes," answered the woman nervously. She raised up on her elbows understanding that she needed to sign the form that Diana was holding out to her. At that instant she saw the instrument resembling long silver pointy tongs with which Elise would grasp the cervix and in Elise's other hand she saw the approximately three and a half inch long spinal needle attached to the thirty-five cc syringe. She promptly passed out cold.

"I don't know whether it is hypotension or panic which made her faint. Check her blood pressure again. Let's get this done quickly, couldn't have better anesthesia." Elise joked feebly. "I'll document that she gave us verbal consent."

Elise lifted up the opening to the womb and slid the long needle down to pierce the area behind the uterus. In this manner, she entered the pelvis and dark blood entered her syringe with minimal effort. Elise expelled the blood into a basin to see if it would clot. She explained to Jack that this would help distinguish between fresh blood accidentally withdrawn from an artery or vein and blood which had collected in the pelvis secondary to the burst tubal pregnancy.

The OB-Gyne resident stepped into Room Ten, looked past Dr. Patel, and peered over Ms. Curtis' right leg which was being held up in the stirrup by Ann. She saw the contents of the basin and said, "Ectopic, I presume."

"Very astute," Elise said without taking her eyes off the liquid blood.

"Jack, can you hold this leg, too, so I can take that blood pressure?" Ann requested.

"Let me get that for you," Sheila, the resident, offered as she grabbed the black cuff off the wall. She pumped it up and then repeated her measurement to be certain.

"It's only eighty over forty," Sheila shared. "We'd better get this lady to the O.R. She's going to be in for a rude awakening, in the Recovery Room, that is."

With that, Sheila hustled out of the examining room to contact her attending and the operating suite staff to arrange the surgery. The emergency nurses packaged Ms. Curtis and Elise went out to the waiting room to inform her family.

Elise stepped through the double glass doors and announced, "The family of Miss Curtis?"

She waited and called out again. No response and then, as she turned around to go back into the E.D., she came face to face, okay, not exactly, more like belly-button to face, with a small child holding an infant in her right arm and the hand of another toddler in her left hand. Elise kneeled and gently spoke to her.

"Hi there, I'm Doctor Elise. And who are you?"

"Tonisha Juno Curtis," she responded in a sweet tiny voice.

"And who is this?" Elise asked as she cradled the infant's chin in her hand and poked the little boy's tummy.

"Dewan Tyla and Hermanina Keesha," Tonisha stated as she swayed her narrow hips back and forth to rock the baby.

"Who is with you?" Elise asked as she glanced around the waiting room, expecting an adult to join her little crowd momentarily.

"My momma. She's sick," Tonisha answered.

"How old are you, sweetie?" Elise asked, afraid of the response.

"Six," stated the little girl proudly. Elise smiled inwardly. It was her experience that up until the age of about four, children were physically unable to verbally tell you how old they were, but instead had to demonstrate with a show of fingers. It always amused her.

"Tonisha, honey, there is no one else here with you except your momma?" she questioned, hoping she was not comprehending the situation correctly.

Tonisha shook her head and Hermanina lifted her hand to her mouth and started to suck greedily and loudly.

Elise sighed. This was a bag of worms she definitely did not want to open. Elise stood and gently took the infant from the child. She offered her right hand to Tonisha who accepted it willingly and they walked back into the main department.

Elise approached the clerk's desk.

"Oh, Michey, could you page social services for me?" she asked in a singsong voice.

The charge nurse walked up behind the group and laughed. "Elise, it looks right on you. You better find yourself a man and fast!"

Elise looked at her disgustedly and thrust the baby into her outstretched arms. "Looks better on you, Leslee. These are Miss Curtis' kids who were out in the waiting room alone. Have the social worker handle it. Doctor Pinchon's films await me. Tonisha, honey, this is Nurse Leslee and she wants to be your friend. You can go with her, it's okay."

Elise reviewed the radiographs and was relieved to note that there was no fracture and the shoulder joint was back where it belonged. The resident carried the folder to Dr. Pinchon's room to share the films with him. He was back to normal, thanks to the miracle of modern medicine and short acting drugs, and was perusing his paper again. That reminded Elise she wanted to call Eric.

"Thank you, dear. It's been a pleasure as always," the elderly gentleman said with a charming smile.

"You're welcome, Doctor Pinchon. Don't come back unless it's just to drop off candy or donuts, y'hear?" and she winked.

Elise stepped into the lounge and dialed Eric's number. He wasn't home so she left a message on his machine.

"Eric, it's me. Meet me at the public library at two o'clock tomorrow. I have an idea."


The emergency resident picked up the next chart waiting to be seen. She rolled her eyes. '*Weakness*' was the chief complaint. She read the triage note further. Mr. Kostanov had been seen at Northwestern Memorial Hospital downtown earlier that day. He was discharged to follow-up with his private physician, but came to C.G.H. for a second opinion instead.

"Mister Kostanov, I am Doctor Silver," Elise said as she held her hand out to greet her new charge.

She realized something was amiss immediately. Mr. Kostanov had the grip of a frail sixteen-year-old Victorian damsel in distress, instead of the steel mill worker he resembled. In fact, Elise noted on the chart that Mr. Kostanov owned his own construction company.

"What seems to be the problem today?" she asked, inviting him to tell her the whole story.

Even his voice was weak as he told her the sequence of events. The day previously he had begun feeling easily fatigued and today was so weak that he couldn't stand in the shower.

"Are you feeling weak all over, or just your legs? Is it worse on one side or the other?" Elise delved.

It seemed to be his legs at first, but now his arms were weak, too. No, he wasn't feeling short of breath.

"How did you know?" Mr. Kostanov asked wonderingly when Elise asked if he had recently had a cold or flu.

Elise examined Mr. Kostanov carefully. She ordered a panel of labs and asked the respiratory therapist to evaluate him. If her suspicions were correct, he could be in serious trouble.

"Jack, you are one lucky intern today!" Elise declared. "You've seen some pretty cool things today, and I'm not done with you yet. Go talk to Mister Kostanov in Room Five. You have five minutes, and then report back to me."

Jack dutifully went into Mr. Kostanov's room and returned in a short time.

"What is your differential diagnosis?" Elise prodded.

"Botulism, myasthenia gravis, hypocalcemia or some other metabolic abnormality,..." Jack listed.

"Good," Elise responded. "What do you think it is, though?"

"I've never seen it before, but does he have Guillain-Barré syndrome?" Jack guessed.

"That's what I think! He's somewhat weak in the upper extremities and very weak in his legs. He has essentially no reflexes and it followed a febrile illness. What do we have to be most concerned about?" Elise questioned.

"Well, don't you have to worry about respiratory failure?" Jack recalled from medical school.

"Exactly! That is the most common reason for these patients to die. Right now his ventilatory parameters are okay, but they need to be closely monitored. We need to admit him and I think step-down or even MICU would be the best place for him," Elise concluded.

"Thanks for showing me all this stuff, Elise. This *has* been a great shift!" Jack acknowledged.


The end of the shift was just as busy as the beginning of the shift but it was well worth it when Sheila called from the labor and delivery suite to let Elise know that Ms. Curtis had made it.

"She had a liter of blood in her belly, but she's stabilized now."

"Thanks for the feedback, I'll let the staff know," Elise acknowledged.

Late period + abdominal pain + fainting from low blood pressure = tubal pregnancy until proven otherwise. It was a pretty safe bet that Phyllis, the newly indoctrinated triage nurse, would never forget that, the lesson of the day. Thank heavens Ms. Curtis didn't have to be sacrificed to teach it to her, Elise thought.

# CHAPTER 18

Her breath made steady puffs of steam despite the scarf she wound about her face as she waited for Eric to show up. He met her on the stairs of the Harold Washington Public Library and berated Elise for not waiting inside.

"I would have found you, you goof! You could catch your death of cold out here," he admonished as he swept her shivering frame inside.

Elise decided to enjoy his concern, rather than explain it was an old wives' tale that people catch colds from being chilled. She stripped off her heavy down coat, her matching hat, scarf and gloves and set them down on a chair near the reference books. Eric's outerwear joined hers and he stood, ready for action.

"So what exactly are we doing here?" he inquired, no longer able to contain his curiosity.

Elise pulled out a chair and motioned Eric to do the same. She produced a pad and pen from her pocketbook and started grilling him.

"Okay, what was the date that your grandfather died on?"

"August twenty-fourth," he answered without hesitation.

Elise wrote this down. She referred to the calendar at the back of her checkbook register and wrote, -*Thursday* next to the date. She cocked her head and nibbled on the pen cap as she thought.

"The lottery is held on Wednesdays and Saturdays, right?"

Eric shook his head up and down, still looking a bit puzzled.

"So the results are printed in the paper on the following days, Thursdays and Sundays?" she double-checked.

"Yup," he confirmed.

She nodded and then rewrote *August 23, 2000* underneath in large block letters and circled it twice.

"You said your grandfather always played the same numbers in the lottery. Do you recall what they were?" Elise's beautiful green eyes glittered with excitement. She held her breath, for if Eric did not know the numbers, and they couldn't find an old ticket stashed away at home, her idea was useless.

"Sure. He played my birthday, June second,..."

Elise wrote *two* under the encircled date.

"his birthday, January fifteenth, my grandmother's birthday, May twenty-fourth,..."

Elise wrote a *fifteen* and a *twenty-four* next to the *two*.

"my father's birthday, September thirtieth. He didn't want to be too heavy on the low numbers so he used our street address, Forty-nine Stanton Place."

Elise reviewed her list: *two*, *fifteen*, *twenty-four*, *thirty*, and *forty-nine*. She wrinkled her forehead, "Wait a minute. There's only five numbers here. The lottery has six."

Eric chuckled. "PopPop always said there were two consecutive numbers so he threw in number sixteen for good measure."

"Okay. Now we're set," Elise said.

She took his hand and led him to the section of the library where newspapers on microfiche resided, taking long strides to cover the ground rapidly.

Elise acquainted herself with the system and eventually located the Chicago Tribune from August 24, 2000. She scanned until she located the section which contained the results from the lottery held on Wednesday, August 23. She compared the numbers: *eight, eleven, twenty-nine, thirty-three, thirty-four, forty-two*.

"See, consecutive numbers. PopPop sure knew his stuff," Eric admired.

Elise could not hide her disappointment. The numbers did not even remotely match. She crumpled up the paper and put it in her pocket.

Eric noticed the look on her face. "Honey, it's okay. Maybe we should let it rest. Or maybe you should express your concerns to the authorities now."

Discouraged, Elise agreed and they retrieved their winter coats and accessories.


"What would you like to do now?" Eric asked as he lifted his eyebrows in a lecherous fashion relaying his vote for the afternoon's activities.

"Sorry, luv, I have to get shoes for tonight," she begged off. "Maybe next year."

Eric smiled and drove to Water Tower Place. To cheer Elise up, Eric bought her a Mrs. Field's white chocolate macadamia nut cookie with about a billion calories in it. When that didn't work, he rode up and down in the glass elevator with her, people watching. Finally, two pair of shoes on a *buy one, get the second pair half price sale*, one compact disk, and one hundred and eighty dollars later, Elise felt better.

At five o'clock, Elise asked Eric to drive her home so she could get gussied up for the New Year's Eve party at Dr. Romano's. He kissed her goodbye with soft, moist lips and promised her there were more where that one came from. She vowed to collect and scurried into the lobby, turning around at the door to wave.


Elise laid out her evening attire. It was a gorgeous emerald green sequined gown with spaghetti straps which hugged her body, and was guaranteed to make Eric want to do the same. It had a short matching jacket and Elise set out two pair of sheer glittery black pantyhose (a good E.M. doctor is like a boy scout, always prepared just in case one developed a run). Her new black high heels were not too high, but beautifully accentuated the definition of her calf muscles. They had a small circle of rhinestones on the toes which tied in with her cubic zirconia and rhinestone jewelry. Elise ran a hot scented bubble bath, poured herself a glass of Chardonnay and stripped down. She winced as she stepped into the tub, the water was almost too hot to bear, but she quickly accommodated. Elise luxuriated, reveling in the melodious crisp sound of the new Joe

Sample C.D. she had purchased today, thinking she must share it with Eric.

Her mind wandered and, as it did so often lately, came to rest on Eric. She smiled, her eyelids relaxed and her arms subconsciously crossed across her chest in a gentle hug mimicking Eric's hold. She thought of his laughing blue eyes and his sexy smile. She really wished she could solve this mystery for him.

A slight frown crossed her face as her attention shifted to Jefferey Weber. *Did Dr. Romano actually murder his long time patient and friend? If so, why? How?* Elise thought to herself, *if I were going to kill someone, I'd plan it carefully. I'd certainly use something that wouldn't show up on autopsy, just in case. I'd use....*

"Oh my God!!!" she exclaimed out loud. Even Fluffers looked startled on the queen-sized bed which could be seen from the doorway of the bathroom.

Elise jumped out of the bathtub and dried off hurriedly. She frantically raced around the bathroom, forcing herself to settle down long enough to blow-dry her hair properly. She was, after all, going to a very fancy party and wanted to look stunning when they rang in the new year. She hoped he would be unable to imagine ringing in any other year without her.

She threw on the pair of jeans she had been wearing earlier and a sweater, foregoing a bra in her extreme haste.

She paced back and forth in her bedroom, and then ran into the living room and booted up her computer. Cursing herself for not being more adept, she tried surfing the net. Refusing to sift through two hundred and sixty-five matches on Yahoo!, she impatiently thought to herself, *What am I going to do, the library is closed?! C'mon, think! That was it!*

She grabbed her down coat and skipped the hat because she had no interest in going to a formal gala with hat-head. She rushed out the door of her apartment and cursed the elevator for being so pokey. She was antsy all the way down and practically ran down some neighbor she knew only cursorily as the doors opened.

"Sorry," she murmured breathlessly as she nearly mowed down an exotic looking black woman in a nursing uniform while racing for the front door.

She ran the three blocks as if her life depended on it. She flung open the door of the 7-11 causing the little bells to jingle signaling a new customer and stepped up to the counter.

"Excuse me, sir, where do you keep the results of old lotteries?" she asked the tall Hindu behind the register who was trying, unsuccessfully, to grow a beard. She prayed they went back far enough.

"Right here, young lady," he answered in a high pitched voice with his crisp British accent. He showed Elise a column on which pages and pages of old lottery numbers bound at the top were affixed.

Desperately she flipped through the months. She reached August and found the twenty-third. She looked above and found the results of the August nineteenth lottery. Her hands were trembling as she fished in her front pocket for the piece of paper. She smoothed out the wrinkles and carefully compared the numbers.

"*Two, fifteen, sixteen, twenty-four, thirty, forty-nine*," she read incredulously as she looked from scrap paper to official results. Elise grabbed the counter and clung to it with all her might. She heard the blood rushing in her ears and her vision grew a little blurry in the periphery. Her heart was pounding like a bass drum and four times as fast.

"I can't believe it! They match! Mister Weber actually hit the jackpot. When Doctor Romano checked the numbers for him that Sunday, he realized he had won the thirty-eight million-dollar lottery. He must have lied to the old man and swiped the winning ticket. He needed a few days to plan the murder, that's why it wasn't the August twenty-third results we looked at earlier today!" Elise muttered aloud.

"Excuse me, miss?" the Indian asked politely.

"Sir, I need this page. Do you have a xerox machine?" she requested.

"What is the date?" He examined the page. "Oh, I don't see why you couldn't take that with you."

"Thank you *so* much!" Elise gushed. She carefully folded it and put it in her pocket, making a mental note to remember to bring it with her to the party.

She flew home the way she came and had to shower again anyway after getting all perspired from the run and the excitement. She finished her preparations and sat down, planning what she would do next. She couldn't *wait* to tell Eric!

# CHAPTER 19

"Great, I'll see you there!" Elise said to Janice.
*Boy, am I glad we aren't wearing the same thing*, she thought. Two years previously she and the director of the department in which she worked accidentally wore very similar dresses to a formal function. They were unable to be seated near one another, and everyone teased them about looking like they should be singing back-up for a rhythm and blues group.

Elise put her lipstick in her black clutch purse and closed it definitively. She donned her dressy winter cape, which was quite fashionable but left a little to desire in the warmth department, and went downstairs to wait for Eric to arrive.

She gracefully climbed into the passenger seat and carefully clasped the seatbelt. She outlined what she had discovered.

"Somehow we have to find proof, Eric!"

"I don't like this a bit, Elise. Why can't we let the police do this? What if it's true? What if he gets violent?"

"What if it's true? Eric, it *has* to be. There is no other explanation. The problem is there is no objective proof, and he knows it. There is no other way," and Eric could tell from the tone of her voice that she had made up her stubborn mind and there was no changing it.

They arrived at Eric's building and parked in his garage. They walked through the house and out into the frigid night air. Eric and Elise pulled their collars closed. Elise walked gingerly, looking to avoid icy spots, afraid she might slip in her new black heels.

Dr. Romano's house certainly stood out on the block tonight. There were hundreds of multicolored Christmas lights bedazzling the entire facade. A large sign out front informed guests that valet service was available. The red uniformed parking attendants were clearly being kept active by the steady stream of arriving partygoers.

This was going to be one hell of a New Year's Eve bash! What a shame they weren't going to be able to fully enjoy their first one together.

The young doctor and her handsome escort stomped the snow off their feet and shucked their overcoats. As they entered, a very formal, white-gloved butler accepted the invitation and took Elise's wrap and Eric's coat. He gave Eric a coat check number.

Elise looked around in awe. Dr. Romano had obviously invested quite a pretty penny in his surroundings. Elise hoped he hadn't already squandered all of Eric's inheritance, for Eric's sake!

The foyer had a beautiful antique hand-carved table of mahogany and hanging above it was either a genuine or a damn good copy of a Monet. There was a huge chandelier hanging above, from the third floor ceiling, sending rainbows of light cascading down. Directly to the left and right, marble stairs spiraled up and up and up. A gorgeous grandfather clock stood patiently ticking away the minutes next to the left staircase. A statue of a woman holding a child stood atop a pedestal on the right.

"He's done a bit of redecorating since Linda died," Eric whispered bitterly in her left ear.

On the foyer table was a large sign which proclaimed welcome and happy New Year to all. In the center, rested a thick Lucite pentagon with a xeroxed copy of the winning lottery ticket embedded in it like a bulgy-eyed fly in golden amber.

"Elise, I've got to look at the ticket," Eric said urgently.

He picked it up and scrutinized it. There it was, in black and white, "*Two, fifteen, sixteen, twenty-four, thirty, forty-nine.*" And in the middle of the ticket, the date, *August 19, 2000*. Eric brushed his fingers over the top as though he could actually make contact with the ticket within.

"It's hard to believe..." he muttered and then he noticed the faint impression, in careful block printing, of 8/19 at the top, above the word, LOTTO. A guttural sound emanated from deep inside him. Elise grabbed Eric's arm to see what was disturbing him so.

"PopPop always scribbled the date on the top, in large numbers so he could tell which ticket was this week's. That's his handwriting, Elise. I would know it anywhere! I can't believe we were right," he said incredulously and shook his head. "That son of a bitch pretended to be our friend, but he murdered my grandfather!"

Eric looked deep into Elise's eyes. His words pierced her very soul as he vowed, "We have to make him pay for it."

Silently she nodded. She wrapped her arms around him as if her strength and love could stop his pain and trembling.

As they walked down the long hallway, Eric pointed out the improvements that Doc Tony had made to his once modest home. He had expanded up and out and was only bound by the size of his Chicago land-lot and his imagination.

The guest list would have read like a Who's Who in Chicago. The mayor and his wife, several aldermen and their spouses, and numerous other heavy-hitters in politics, business, and society in general, were present. There were many physicians from Chicago General Hospital, and the "old boys' club" was especially well represented. Elegant black-bedecked waitresses with frilly white starched aprons and long white gloves milled about like angry bees protecting their hive, offering a host of hot and cold hors d'oeuvres.

The first room to the right was the library. It housed hundreds of books, medical, fiction, rare and precious tomes. There was an expensive oriental rug on the floor under two leather sofas and a recliner. A beautiful peek-a-boo fireplace was radiating heat and making inviting popping sounds.

"This room is gorgeous, Eric. Can't you picture us snuggled in front of the fire on a cold snowy winter's Sunday reading the newspaper?"

Eric didn't answer although he did give her hand a squeeze. Several attending physicians from C.G.H. greeted Elise and she wished them a happy New Year in return.

They peered into the next room. A mammoth home entertainment unit flanked the other side of the peek-a-boo fireplace. A huge, state-of-the-art JVC television set was ensconced in an oddly shaped space flanked by magnificent glass art pieces. Obviously Dr. Romano's interior designer was preparing for the era of digital television. Surround sound was issuing forth Wynton Marsalis from the CD player.

Janice and Don were sharing a moment in front of the fire. They waved Eric and Elise over.

"Jan told me you've been acting weird, even weirder than usual," Don said in a gruff, but loving, big brother tone of voice. "What is going on?"

Janice was quiet but her eyes reflected her concern. "I'm sorry, 'Lise. I told him not to say anything, but he doesn't listen to *me* either!" Her apology was halfhearted and her relief that it was out was clear.

Elise dragged them into an unoccupied corner and summed up the whole story.

"You know, he's been pretty creepy since Doctor Morris died," Janice observed. "He's been a little forward, if you know what I mean. I've just been dismissing it."

"Well, we're going to look for evidence," Elise declared.

"I would advise against that. You should make a report and let the legal system handle this. You could get into real trouble," Don warned.

"Don, I don't expect you to get involved, but this is something we have to do," Elise replied firmly. They all knew how futile it was to try to talk his headstrong sister out of anything, once she had set her mind to do it. "We'll see you later. Let us know how the food was. It looks fabulous, but I'm afraid it would give us indigestion to eat Doctor Romano's food."

"Don't get into trouble," Don warned.

"We'll try not to," Elise conceded.

They continued into what normally was a massive living room. The furniture had been rearranged and a dance floor had been laid down. The decorations were glitzy and colored lights bounced everywhere. The six piece band in the corner completed the transformation into a ballroom. Segueing from Mozart to big band tunes to Andrew Lloyd Webber, they had everyone up and dancing. Elise thought it was a shame she wasn't going to get to enjoy this party. She did love a good dance.

Finally they spotted him. Dr. Romano was in the far corner chatting with several hospital board members and the chairman of the department of family practice. He sported an expensive black tuxedo splashed with a touch of burgundy in the cummerbund and bow tie. His teeth looked like polished ivory against his olive skin as he laughed effortlessly with his colleagues.

"Why don't you stay here as a lookout?" Eric suggested.

"Because you have no idea what you're looking for, for one thing. Why don't *you* stay here?" she retorted.

He leaned down and kissed her softly on her full lips.

"Okay, we're in this together. Let's go upstairs to the office. If there is going to be any evidence, that's where it would be," he agreed.

"Ready as I'll ever be!" she declared and they proceeded.

# CHAPTER 20

The food sure did smell heavenly as they quickly traversed the hallway past the kitchen. The dining room had tables set up for serving the food.

"It looks good, but it would defile PopPop's memory to eat this devil's food," Eric growled.

They made their way up the spiral staircase. Elise was awed at the artwork. Some of those pieces were worth twice and thrice her yearly salary, and even then some.

The first room to the right of the stairs was the office. As she entered the room, her attention was immediately drawn to a heavy dark wood desk with ornately carved legs located against the wall between two windows. Papers were stacked in neat piles on top and Elise noted a small hand held dictating recorder on one of the piles of patient folders. There was an expensive Mont Blanc pen and pencil set in a genuine white marble stand in front. A brass lamp with a stained glass shade stood atop and sent colorful bytes of light on the paneled walls. In the right hand corner perched a clock which was ten minutes fast. A sophisticated computer system with a zip drive and writable CD-ROM was in the middle of the desk.

"This was Linda's computer. Doc Tony probably doesn't have a clue what to do with it. He is a completely computer-illiterate fossil. I'm going to log on and see what I find," Eric decided.

He flipped on the power switch and started punching keys on the keyboard.

"Well, he hasn't changed Linda's password," Eric informed Elise.

"How do you know it?" Elise asked curiously.

"We spent a lot of time in here, surfing the 'net, just fooling around."

Elise didn't answer.

"Not fooling around like *that*!" Eric explained, in mock indignation.

She continued to survey the room. There was a closet to the left of the entrance and file cabinets for papers and x-rays against the wall to the right. An illuminated board to view films was behind the leather swivel desk chair. The final wall had a large bookcase and a door.

Elise peeked through the door. It led to the master bathroom, which could also be entered from the master suite. She left the door ajar so if someone entered the bathroom, they would know.

"I'm going to look in the closet. I want to see if I can find any medications that Romano used on your grandfather," Elise offered.

"Mmhmnn," Eric absently answered, already engrossed in the words on the screen.

Elise switched on the light and stepped into the closet. There were lab coats hanging up on hooks. Stacks of office supplies were next to a small safe on the floor to the right of the door. Elise searched the floor. Peeking from behind the safe was the corner of a radiograph folder. There was no label on the front. Elise assumed it would be a set of copies, because that was how they were usually stored. Her heart skipped a beat when she slid the films out and held them up to the light.

These were the original C.T. scans of one Jefferey Weber, taken on August 24, 2000. All they showed was some brain shrinkage. No bleed shaped like any continent, no abnormality. No reason for him to die at all. Linda must have taken the original films from the technologist and substituted her doctored ones to be brought over to the emergency department.

As she lowered the films, her eyes lingered above and she scrutinized the contents on the shelf. She immediately recognized the traditional doctor's black bag pushed way in the back. Rummaging around to find something to stand on, Elise found a step stool. She dragged it over and reached up for the bag.

Inside was a wide selection of pill bottles and liquids. The contents read like a pharmacy - antidepressants, AIDS medications, narcotics, blood pressure medicine. There was insulin and numerous antibiotics. The labels reflected the fact that Doc Tony had collected the medicine from many different patients over a long period of time.

"Boy, if he's been donating medication all along, imagine how much he had before!" Elise wondered aloud quietly.

She found a bottle with Haldol in it. The date on it was 5/15/00. Circumstantial at best, but Elise was convinced that this could have been the inciting factor in Mr. Weber's "stroke." As for the cause of death, Dr. Romano had numerous vials in his bag which could have been injected to cause death, but would have been undetectable on autopsy.

Exiting the treasure trove of evidence, Elise called for Eric's attention, "Look what I found."

She placed the black bag on the desk and then clipped the C.T. films on the viewbox and pointed to the name. The technologist's number was one-sixteen. She was going to show Eric the medications when he interrupted her.

"Look what *I* found," he said.


He gave up the desk chair so Elise could sit in front of the computer screen. Chills went up her spine as she read the last entry of a dead woman.

*Dear Diary,*

*I don't know how much longer I can take this. I can't believe I ever wanted things to work out with that monster. He scared me so much about how deeply he had gotten us into debt with his damn gambling, that I helped him. I loved him so much once, but now I can't stand being in the same zip code as him.*

*Eric, on the other hand, is the most wonderful man I've ever known. He's embarrassed by how much I care for him, but he's always so kind and compassionate towards me. How can I ever make up for what I've done to him? How I've betrayed his friendship. He loved his grandfather so much and I helped take him away. Maybe*

*I should tell him. He'll hate me, but at least I'll be able to live with myself again.*

*What irony! I haven't been able to eat for weeks and I've lost 15 pounds. I look thinner and better that I ever have, but I hate myself so much. I have no energy at work, but I can't sleep at night. The nightmares won't go away.*

*I've made my decision. I have to do it. Tony may be able to live with this, but I can't.*

*I feel better already.*

It ended. Elise was speculating on exactly what she meant. *Was she planning to confess? Did Dr. Romano murder her too to keep his secret? Or had she decided to commit suicide?*

The door closed quietly. The startled couple looked up and were alarmed to see Dr. Romano not ten feet in front of them. He wasn't smiling now. In fact, he looked pretty darn menacing.

"What do you think you are doing in my private study?" he growled.

Elise stood up from the chair and reflexively inched over next to Eric. She sat on the edge of the desk and leaned on the stacks of patient files. Dr. Romano cornered the two in the confines of the desk as he took the swivel chair and scanned the monitor screen.

"Did you kill her, too?" Eric asked venomously.

Dr. Romano chuckled. "No, that sniveling coward couldn't take the guilt. She really did do herself in."

"But you could take the guilt, couldn't you? You killed Mister Weber," Elise spelled it out.

"My dear, I can tolerate a lot for thirty-eight million dollars," he replied.

"I'm sorry. I just can't understand murdering someone you've been friends with for many years, for money," Elise's voice dripped contempt with the last phrase.

"Actually, I try to think of it more as self-preservation. You see, I have a bit of a gambling problem. I got us pretty deep into debt out in Vegas and the fellas were anxious to have their money back. They were threatening me with quite unpleasant things."

Dr. Romano turned to Eric and said, "If it's any consolation, I did feel bad, but I looked at it as your grandfather or me."

Elise clarified it, "So when you realized Jefferey Weber had hit the lottery jackpot, you planned it all. You gave him some Haldol in his breakfast which gave him a dystonic reaction. Since he wasn't supposed to be on any meds like that, you anticipated that we would be suspecting a stroke."

"It was fortunate that he reacted that way. If he had just gotten very drowsy from the sedative effects, it would have had the same outcome," Dr. Romano pointed out.

"You already had had Linda find a brain scan that showed a bleed incompatible with life. For a computer whiz like her, it was a piece of cake to superimpose Mister Weber's data on the nasty scan," Elise continued speculating. "But how did you actually kill him? Did you use insulin? Or what?"

"I often stop in to see my patients in the E.R. if I know they are there. It was simple enough to give him a massive shot of potassium after Eric had left. Since he wasn't put back on the monitor yet after returning from the bathroom, it was some time before the nurse noted he was dead. I, of course, was long gone from the scene."

"Doc Tony, how could you?" Eric asked rhetorically.

"Tell me, how did you figure this all out?" Dr. Romano asked.

"I guess serendipity works for the good guys too sometimes," Elise responded. "I was looking for C.T. cases for radiology conference and thought it was odd to have two identical brain scans. Of course, now you're screwed because we have plenty of evidence to have you put away forever."

"Oh, I'm sorry, dear. Did I give you the mistaken idea that I was going to let the two of you ruin my life?" the older physician asked facetiously.

His left hand had sidled into the upper left-hand drawer of the desk and exited with a small pistol in it.

"Did you notice the safe in the closet where you stole my radiographs from? There is a lot of valuable jewelry in there. I bought this gun to protect my home," he explained as he removed the safety and prepared the gun for firing.

"Oh, like how would you possibly explain shooting us, here, at your party?" Elise taunted.

"First of all, I am going to give you an alternative," Dr. Romano began and Eric interrupted him.

"Wait, Doc Tony, you can have the money. Just don't hurt Elise," he pleaded.

"I'm sorry, Eric, but the two of you really can't be trusted to keep this secret. There's just too much at stake. However, I was going to give you the option of going in a more pleasant fashion. I have lots of morphine in this bag of tricks," he said as he patted his doctor's bag setting on the desk. "I will be happy to let you inject yourselves, or each other, with a lethal overdose. It probably would be considerably less painful than a gunshot."

Elise snorted skeptically.

"And how, pray tell, would you explain away two bloody dead bodies in the middle of this party?" she asked.

"Who do you think will hear anything all the way up here? We are light-years away from the rest of the party guests. I'll tell you again, thirty eight million dollars is a lot of money. Even after paying off my debts and Uncle Sam and spending a little bit on redecorating, I still have more than enough to pay off Jake in the coroner's office to fudge the time of death a bit.

"The two of you sneaks must have cased this joint during the party and you waited until everyone left. Then you came in this room to try to crack open the safe."

Dr. Romano laughed a maniacal laugh as he opened his doctor's case and whipped out a stethoscope. He waved it about.

"You must have seen too many movies and thought you could hear the tumblers with this piece of equipment. Naturally, since I was retiring to bed, and my bathroom is adjacent to this room, I heard you. I quietly took my gun from my bedroom nightstand and accosted you. You went berserk and attacked me."

He thought for a moment. "I shot you first, Eric, because you rushed me. You...I'll just tell the authorities that I don't even know your name, although I have seen you around C.G.H. I always notice the pretty ones."

"Fuck you, Tony," Eric spat.

Dr. Romano continued as if he hadn't even heard him.

"You ran at me next. In fact, after you are dead, I think I'll scratch myself in the face with your fingernails. The pieces of flesh under your nails will be a realistic touch, don't you think, Elise?"

"Do you really want to know what I think?" Elise asked.

His reverie interrupted, Dr. Romano's eyes narrowed as he focused on Elise.

"What?" he baited her.

"I think you are insane. Greedy and insane. Evil, greedy, and certifiably nuts," she answered. "And I know that you will never get away with it. My brother is a cop and he will know that it is all a lie. He knows I would never do any of those things you are saying. And he won't rest until the truth is out," the fiery resident finished defiantly.

"Ah, what a waste. You remind me of my late wife in her idealistic days. You should have taken that job I arranged to have you offered at the Cleveland Clinic and given up this fool's quest.

"But I assure you, all the evidence you have found will be gone minutes after you two are dead. Your brother will never be able to figure this out, let alone prove it. But it's time for you to choose. The bloody messy death, or the euphoric one? I'm not all bad. I'll even give you a moment to say goodbye."


Eric took Elise in his arms and pulled her close. He brushed his fingers across her right cheek where a tear had silently coursed down.

"I'm so sorry," he murmured.

"What are you talking about? This is all my fault. I should never have dragged you into this," she countered bravely.

He tipped her face up and gently kissed her salty lips. The kiss grew and became more urgent and passionate.

"Elise, I love you," Eric declared in her ear.

"I love you, too," she answered.

"Oh, how touching," Doc Tony sneered. "Have you chosen? Do you want to shoot or be shot?" He giggled at his cleverness.

"I have a better idea. Put down that gun, or that expensive rug is going to be soaked in your blood," a voice boomed from the bathroom door.

Don was standing in the doorway. His near black hair was tousled and his cheeks were flushed. His sienna eyes looked wild and he had an unmistakably determined look on his face. His rented tuxedo was unbuttoned to give him access to his gun which, as usual, had been holstered on his hip. He was holding his gun in his right hand, steadying it with his left hand. It was pointed directly at Dr. Romano.

Elise thought her big brother had never looked so good in her whole life. Uncontrollably, a giggle emerged from her gut.

"Doctor Romano, may I introduce you to my brother, Don Silver? I'm quite sure you will not be pleased to make his acquaintance, because he is a police officer and I believe he's a bit peeved that you were planning on offing his favorite older younger sister," she rattled off, her composure returning now that it looked like she was being rescued. Obviously Don knew that Elise never listened to anyone's advice.

Dr. Romano slowly lowered his piece and placed it on the desk deliberately. Eric lurched forward and grabbed it. Don slowly approached the older physician and used his left hand to remove his handcuffs from somewhere inside his tux.

"You'll still never be able to prove anything. You don't have an eyewitness who will corroborate your ridiculous accusations," Dr. Romano blustered.

Elise giggled again from the absurdity of it all. Her right hand picked up the small Lanier tape recorder which Dr. Romano used to dictate his notes for his secretary to type. She rewound a few seconds and pressed play.

"Oh, how touching," they heard Doc Tony's voice. "Have you chosen? Do you want to shoot or be shot?" A maniacal giggle.

"I have a better idea. Put down that gun, or that expensive rug is going to be soaked in your blood," Don's voice replayed. Then a woman's nervous giggle and the recording ended.

"I got the whole thing," the resident informed her brother.

"Great thinking!" he acknowledged.

Dr. Romano buried his face in his hands, recognizing his defeat.

"And my date and I came up here to your bedroom to fool around a bit and we just happened to overhear the whole thing ourselves. I figure we should make pretty formidable corroborating witnesses, don't you agree?" Don added.

Don slapped the cuffs on Dr. Romano and began informing him of his rights. After he finished, he turned his attention to Elise.

"Are you all right?" he asked protectively.

"I sure am now! Thank you," she answered.

Janice peeped her head in from the bathroom.

"Well, I'm not. Hurry up. It's almost time," she pouted.

"Babe, I think I'm going to have to owe you one," Don said apologetically.

Indignantly, Janice replied, "Can't you just cuff him to a chair or bedpost or something? Just 'til midnight?"

"I do have to call for backup. You can stay with me until they come," he compromised.

"Don, we're going to go back to Eric's and get changed. I assume you need us to come down to the station and make a report," Elise said.

"Yeah. Don't take any of the evidence with you. I'll get a search warrant and you can tell me what we need," Don responded.

Elise walked up to her brother, stood on her tiptoes and kissed his cheek solemnly.

"Thanks," she repeated and gave his neck a squeeze. "Happy New Year!"

Eric shook Don's hand and thanked him again. He then took his date's hand and they left the office. Elise was a bit shaky and leaned against him as they descended the marble spiral staircase.

At the bottom of the steps, a waiter stood with a tray of bubbling champagne flutes. Eric took two off the tray, handed one to Elise, and clinked glasses.

"*L'chaim!*" he toasted. The expression, 'To life!', held more meaning tonight than it ever had before.

"To a happy and healthy New Year!" Elise answered.

They tipped the glasses and started sipping the champagne. All of a sudden, the grandfather clock began chiming the hour in a deep reverberant sound.

From way back in the house, the band cued up. Strains of "Auld Lang Syne" wafted down the hallway.

Eric smiled and started down the hallway urgently, tugging at Elise's hand to follow him. He stopped abruptly at the library and entered it. Gulping down the last sip of champagne, Eric took the empty glass and threw it into the fireplace. It shattered.

"I've always wanted to do that!" he admitted giddily.

Elise followed suit and they laughed out loud.

The twelfth bong sounded and the party goers simultaneously shouted, "Happy New Year!"

Eric took Elise in his arms and said, "Happy New Year!"

Elise said, "Happy *real* Millennium!"

And then he gave her a New Year's kiss filled with gratitude and promises.

She softly asserted, "Yes, I think it will be a very good year!"

# ABOUT THE AUTHOR

Erica E. Remer, MD, FACEP, is a board-certified emergency physician who lives in Beachwood, Ohio, and practices half-time at the Cleveland Clinic. She has a husband, Erick, who is an abdominal imaging radiologist, and a brilliant and affectionate son, Scott, who plans to publish his own works someday. When not writing or saving lives, Erica likes cooking gourmet meals and playing Yahtzee with Scott.